5791202   JHABVALA, R.P.
Experience of
823 | SHA   India

F

D1348266

AN EXPERIENCE OF INDIA

In her Introduction to these stories entitled Myself in India, Ruth Prawer Jhabvala describes what it is like to be a foreigner living there, struggling not to be overwhelmed. AN EXPERIENCE OF INDIA is the theme of this collection which is brilliantly conveyed in these short stories.

A

Novels
To Whom She Will
The Nature of Passion
Esmond in India
The Householder
Get Ready for Battle
A Backward Place

Short Stories
Like Birds, like Fishes
A Stronger Climate

An Experience of India

R. PRAWER JHABVALA

JOHN MURRAY

For
Jennifer and Shashi
and
'Bombay Talkie'

© R. PRAWER JHABVALA 1966, 1968, 1971

Printed in Great Britain by
Lewis Reprints Limited,
London and Tonbridge

0 7195 2577 2

CONTENTS

Acknowledgements are due to the *London Magazine*, *The New Yorker*, *Cosmopolitan*, the *Kenyon Review*, *Encounter* and *The Cornhill Magazine* in which these stories first appeared.

Introduction: Myself in India

I have lived in India for most of my adult life. My husband is Indian and so are my children. I am not, and less so every year.

India reacts very strongly on people. Some loathe it, some love it, most do both. There is a special problem of adjustment for the sort of people who come today, who tend to be liberal in outlook and have been educated to be sensitive and receptive to other cultures. But it is not always easy to be sensitive and receptive to India : there comes a point where you have to close up in order to protect yourself. The place is very strong and often proves too strong for European nerves. There is a cycle that Europeans — by Europeans I mean all Westerners, including Americans — tend to pass through. It goes like this : first stage, tremendous enthusiasm — everything Indian is marvellous; second stage, everything Indian not so marvellous; third stage, everything Indian abominable. For some people it ends there, for others the cycle renews itself and goes on. I have been through it so many times that now I think of myself as strapped to a wheel that goes round and round and sometimes I'm up and sometimes I'm down. When I meet other Europeans, I can usually tell after a few moments conversation at what stage of the cycle they happen to be. Everyone likes to talk about India, whether they happen to be loving or loathing it. It is a topic on which a lot of things can be said, and on a variety of aspects — social, economic, political, philosophical :

it makes fascinating viewing from every side.

However, I must admit that I am no longer interested in India. What I am interested in now is myself in India — which sometimes, in moments of despondency, I tend to think of as my survival in India. I had better say straightaway that the reason why I live in India is because my strongest human ties are here. If I hadn't married an Indian, I don't think I would ever have come here for I am not attracted — or used not to be attracted — to the things that usually bring people to India. I know I am the wrong type of person to live here. To stay and endure, one should have a mission and a cause, to be patient, cheerful, unselfish, strong. I am a central European with an English education and a deplorable tendency to constant self-analysis. I am irritable and have weak nerves.

The most salient fact about India is that it is very poor and very backward. There are so many other things to be said about it but this must remain the basis of all of them. We may praise Indian democracy, go into raptures over Indian music, admire Indian intellectuals — but whatever we say, not for one moment should we lose sight of the fact that a very great number of Indians never get enough to eat. Literally that : from birth to death they never for one day cease to suffer from hunger. *Can* one lose sight of that fact? God knows, I've tried. But after seeing what one has to see here every day, it is not really possible to go on living one's life the way one is used to. People dying of starvation in the streets, children kidnapped and maimed to be sent out as beggars — but there is no point in making a catalogue of the horrors with which one lives, *on* which one lives, as on the back of an animal. Obviously, there has to be some adjustment.

There are several ways. The first and best is to be a strong person who plunges in and does what he can as a doctor or social worker. I often think that perhaps this is the only condition under which Europeans have any right to be here. I know several people like that. They are usually attached to some mission. They work very hard and stay very cheerful. Every few years they are sent on home leave. Once I met such a person — a woman doctor — who had just returned from her first home leave after being out here for twelve years. I asked her : but what does it feel like to go back after such a long time? How do you manage to adapt yourself? She didn't understand. This question which was of such tremendous import to me — how to adapt oneself to the differences between Europe and India — didn't mean a thing to her. It simply didn't matter. And she was right, for in view of the things she sees and does every day, the delicate nuances of one's own sensibilities are best forgotten.

Another approach to India's basic conditions is to accept them. This seems to be the approach favoured by most Indians. Perhaps it has something to do with their belief in reincarnation. If things are not to your liking in this life, there is always the chance that in your next life everything will be different. It appears to be a consoling thought for both rich and poor. The rich man stuffing himself on pilao can do so with an easy conscience because he knows he has earned this privilege by his good conduct in previous lives; and the poor man can watch him with some degree of equanimity for he knows that next time round it may well be *he* who will be digging into that pilao while the other will be crouching outside the door with an empty stomach. However, this path of acceptance is not open to you if you don't have a belief in reincarnation ingrained within you. And if you don't accept, then what can you do? Sometimes one wants just to run away and go to a place where everyone has enough to eat and clothes to wear and a home fit to live in. But even when you get there, can you ever forget? Having once seen the sights in India, and the way it has been ordained that people must live out their lives, nowhere in the world can ever be all that good to be in again.

None of this is what I wanted to say. I wanted to concentrate only on myself in India. But I could not do so before indicating the basis on which everyone who comes here has to live. I have a nice house, I do my best to live in an agreeable way. I shut all my windows, I let down the blinds, I turn on the airconditioner; I read a lot of books, with a special preference for the great masters of the novel. All the time I know myself to be on the back of this great animal of poverty and backwardness. It is not possible to pretend otherwise. Or rather, one does pretend, but retribution follows. Even if one never rolls up the blinds and never turns off the airconditioner, something is bound to go wrong. People are not meant to shut themselves up in rooms and pretend there is nothing outside.

Now I think I am drawing nearer to what I want to be my subject. Yes, something is wrong : I am not happy this way. I feel lonely, shut in, shut off. It is my own fault. I should go out more and meet

people and learn what is going on. All right, so I am
not a doctor nor a social worker nor a saint nor at all
a good person; then the only thing to do is to try and
push that aspect of India out of sight and turn to
others. There are many others. I live in the capital
where so much is going on. The winter is one round of
parties, art exhibitions, plays, music and dance recitals,
visiting European artistes : there need never be a dull
moment. Yet all my moments are dull. Why? It is my
own fault, I know. I can't quite explain it to myself
but somehow I have no heart for these things here. Is
it because all the time underneath I feel the animal
moving? But I have decided to ignore the animal. I
wish to concentrate only on modern, Westernised
India, and on modern, well-off, cultured Westernised
Indians.

Let me try and describe a Westernised Indian woman
with whom I ought to have a lot in common and
whose company I ought to enjoy. She has been to
Oxford or Cambridge or some smart American college.
She speaks flawless, easy, colloquial English with a
charming lilt of an accent. She has a degree in
economics or political science or English literature. She
comes from a good family. Her father may have been
an I.C.S. officer or some other high-ranking government official; he too was at Oxford or Cambridge,
and he and her mother travelled in Europe in pre-war
days. They have always lived a Western-style life, with
Western food and an admiration for Western culture.
The daughter now tends rather to frown on this. She
feels one should be more deeply Indian, and with this
end in view, she wears handloom saris and traditional
jewellery and has painted an abnormally large vermilion

mark on her forehead. She is interested in Indian
classical music and dance. If she is rich enough — she
may have married into one of the big Indian business
houses — she will become a patroness of the arts and
hold delicious parties on her lawn on summer nights.
All her friends are there — and she has so many, both
Indian and European, all interesting people — and
trays of iced drinks are carried round by servants in
uniform and there is intelligent conversation and then
there is a superbly arranged buffet supper and more
intelligent conversation, and then the crown of the
evening : a famous Indian maestro performing on the
sitar. The guests recline on carpets and cushions on
the lawn. The sky sparkles with stars and the languid
summer air is fragrant with jasmine. There are many
pretty girls reclining against bolsters; their faces are
melancholy for the music is stirring their hearts, and
sometimes they sigh with yearning and happiness and
look down at their pretty toes (adorned with a tiny
silver toe-ring) peeping out from under the sari. Here
is Indian life and culture at its highest and best. Yet,
with all that, it need not be thought that our hostess
has forgotten her Western education. Not at all. In her
one may see the best of East and West combined. She
is interested in a great variety of topics and can hold
her own in any discussion. She loves to exercise her
emancipated mind, and whatever the subject of conversation — economics, or politics, or literature, or
film — she has a well-formulated opinion on it and
knows how to express herself. How lucky for me if I
could have such a person for a friend! What enjoyable,
lively times we two could have together!

In fact, my teeth are set on edge if I have to listen

to her for more than five minutes — yes, even though everything she says is so true and in line with the most advanced opinions of today. But when she says it, somehow, even though I know the words to be true, they ring completely false. It is merely lips moving and sounds coming out : it doesn't mean anything, nothing of what she says (though she says it with such conviction, skill, and charm) is of the least importance to her. She is only making conversation in the way she knows educated women have to make conversation. And so it is with all of them. Everything they say, all that lively conversation round the buffet table, is not prompted by anything they really feel strongly about but by what they think they ought to feel strongly about. This applies not only to subjects which are naturally alien to them — for instance, when they talk oh so solemnly! and with such profound intelligence! of Godard and Becket and ecology — but when they talk about themselves too. They know Modern India to be an important subject and they have a lot to say about it : but though they themselves *are* Modern India, they don't look at themselves, they are not conditioned to look at themselves except with the eyes of foreign experts whom they have been taught to respect. And while they are fully aware of India's problems and are up on all the statistics and all the arguments for and against nationalisation and a socialistic pattern of society, all the time it is as if they were talking about some *other* place — as if it were a subject for debate — an abstract subject — and not a live animal actually moving under their feet.

But if I have no taste for the company of these Westernised Indians, then what else is there? Other

Indians don't really have a social life, not in our terms; the whole conception of such a life is imported. It is true that Indians are gregarious in so far as they hate to be alone and always like to sit together in groups; but these groups are clan-units — it is the family, or clan-members, who gather together and enjoy each other's company. And again, their conception of enjoying each other's company is different from ours. For them it is enough just to *be* together; there are long stretches of silence in which everyone stares into space. From time to time there is a little spurt of conversation, usually on some commonplace everyday subject such as rising prices, a forthcoming marriage, or a troublesome neighbour. There is no attempt at exercising the mind or testing one's wits against those of others : the pleasure lies only in having other familiar people around and enjoying the air together and looking forward to the next meal. There is actually something very restful about this mode of social inter-course and certainly holds more pleasure than the synthetic social life led by Westernised Indians. It is also more adapted to the Indian climate which invites one to be absolutely relaxed in mind and body, to do nothing, to think nothing, just to feel, to *be*. I have in fact enjoyed sitting around like that for hours on end. But there is something in me that after some time revolts against such lassitude. I can't just *be*! Suddenly I jump up and rush away out of that contented circle. I want to do something terribly difficult like climbing a mountain or reading the *Critique of Pure Reason*. I feel tempted to bang my head against the wall as if to wake myself up. Anything to prevent myself from being sucked down into that bog of passive, intuitive being. I feel I cannot, I must not allow myself to live this way.

Of course there are other Europeans more or less in the same situation as myself. For instance, other women married to Indians. But I hesitate to seek them out. People suffering from the same disease do not usually make good company for one another. Who is to listen to whose complaints? On the other hand, with what enthusiasm I welcome visitors from abroad. Their physical presence alone is a pleasure to me. I love to see their fresh complexions, their red cheeks that speak of wind and rain; and I like to see their clothes and their shoes, to admire the texture of these solid European materials and the industrial skills that have gone into making them. I also like to hear the way in which these people speak. In some strange way their accents, their intonations are redolent to me of the places from which they have come, so that as voices rise and fall I hear in them the wind stirring in English trees or a mild brook murmuring through a summer wood. And apart from these sensuous pleasures, there is also the pleasure of hearing what they have to say. I listen avidly to what is said about people I know or have heard of and about new plays and restaurants and changes and fashions. However, neither the subject nor my interest in it is inexhaustible; and after that, it is my turn. What about India? Now they want to hear, but I don't want to say. I feel myself growing sullen. I don't want to talk about India. There is nothing I can tell them. There is nothing they would understand. However, I do begin to talk, and after a time even to talk with passion. But everything I say is wrong. I listen to myself with horror; they too listen

with horror. I want to stop and reverse, but I can't. I
want to cry out, this is not what I mean! You are
listening to me in entirely the wrong context! But
there is no way of explaining the context. It would
take too long, and anyway what is the point? It's such
a small, personal thing. I fall silent. I have nothing
more to say. I turn my face and want them to go
away.

So I am back again alone in my room with the
blinds drawn and the airconditioner on. Sometimes,
when I think of my life, it seems to have contracted to
this one point and to be concentrated in this one
room, and it is always a very hot, very long afternoon
when the airconditioner has failed. I cannot describe
the *oppression* of such afternoons. It is a physical
oppression — heat pressing down on me and pressing
in the walls and the ceiling and congealing together
with time which has stood still and will never move
again. And it is not only those two — heat and time —
that are laying their weight on me but behind them,
or held within them, there is something more which
I can only describe as the whole of India. This is
hyperbole, but I need hyperbole to express my feelings about those countless afternoons spent over what
now seem to me countless years in a country for which
I was not born. India swallows me up and now it
seems to me that I am no longer in my room but in
the white-hot city streets under a white-hot sky; people
cannot live in such heat so everything is deserted —
no, not quite, for here comes a smiling leper in a cart
being pushed by another leper; there is also the carcase
of a dog and vultures have swooped down on it. The
river has dried up and stretches in miles of flat cracked

earth; it is not possible to make out where the river ceases and the land begins for this too is as flat, as cracked, as dry as the river-bed and stretches on for ever. Until we come to a jungle in which wild beasts live, and then there are ravines and here live outlaws with the hearts of wild beasts. Sometimes they make raids into the villages and they rob and burn and mutilate and kill for sport. More mountains and these are very, very high and now it is no longer hot but terribly cold, we are in snow and ice and here is Mount Kailash on which sits Siva the Destroyer wearing a necklace of human skulls. Down in the plains they are worshipping him. I can see them from here — they are doing something strange — what is it? I draw nearer. Now I can see. They are killing a boy. They hack him to pieces and now they bury the pieces into the foundations dug for a new bridge. There is a priest with them who is quite naked except for ash smeared all over him; he is reciting some holy verses over the foundations, to bless and propitiate.

I am using these exaggerated images in order to give some idea of how intolerable India — the idea, the sensation of it — can become. A point is reached where one must escape, and if one can't do so physically, then some other way must be found. And I think it is not only Europeans but Indians too who feel themselves compelled to seek refuge from their often unbearable environment. Here perhaps less than anywhere else is it possible to believe that this world, this life, is all there is for us, and the temptation to write it off and substitute something more satisfying becomes overwhelming. This brings up the question whether religion is such a potent force in India because

life is so terrible, or is it the other way round — is life
so terrible because, with the eyes of the spirit turned
elsewhere, there is no incentive to improve its quality?
Whichever it is, the fact remains that the eyes of the
spirit *are* turned elsewhere, and it really is true that
God seems more present in India than in other places.
Every morning I wake up at 3a.m. to the sound of
someone pouring out his spirit in devotional song; and
then at dawn the temple bells ring, and again at dusk,
and conch-shells are blown, and there is the smell of
incense and of the slightly overblown flowers that are
placed at the feet of smiling, pink-cheeked idols. I
read in the papers that the Lord Krishna has been
reborn as the son of a weaver woman in a village
somewhere in Madhya Pradesh. On the banks of the
river there are figures in meditation and one of them
may turn out to be the teller in your bank who cashed
your cheque just a few days ago; now he is in the
lotus pose and his eyes are turned up and he is in
ecstasy. There are ashrams full of little old half-starved
widows who skip and dance about, they giggle and
play hide and seek because they are Krishna's milk-
maids. And over all this there is a sky of enormous
proportions — so much larger than the earth on which
you live, and often so incredibly beautiful, an unflawed
unearthly blue by day, all shining with stars at night,
that it is difficult to believe that something grand and
wonderful beyond the bounds of human comprehen-
sion does not emanate from there.

   I love listening to Indian devotional songs. They
seem pure like water drawn from a well; and the
emotions they express are both beautiful and easy to
understand because the imagery employed is so human.

The soul crying out for God is always shown as the beloved yearning for the lover in an easily recognisable way ("I wait for Him. Do you hear His step? He has come"). I feel soothed when I hear such songs and all my discontentment falls away. I see that everything I have been fretting about is of no importance at all because all that matters is this promise of eternal bliss in the Lover's arms. I become patient and good and feel that everything is good. Unfortunately this tranquil state does not last for long, and after a time it again seems to me that nothing is good and neither am I. Once somebody said to me : "Just see, how sweet is the Indian soul that can see God in a cow!" But when I try to assume this sweetness, it turns sour : for, however much I may try and fool myself, whatever veils I may try, for the sake of peace of mind, to draw over my eyes, it is soon enough clear to me that the cow *is* a cow, and a very scrawny, underfed, diseased one at that. And then I feel that I want to keep this knowledge, however painful it is, and not exchange it for some other that may be true for an Indian but can never quite become that for me.

And here, it seems to me, I come to the heart of my problem. To live in India and be at peace one must to a very considerable extent become Indian and adopt Indian attitudes, habits, beliefs, assume if possible an Indian personality. But how is this possible? And even if it were possible — without cheating oneself — would it be desirable? Should one want to try and become something other than what one is? I don't always say no to this question. Sometimes it seems to me how pleasant it would be to say yes and give in and wear a sari and be meek and accepting and

see God in a cow. Other times it seems worth while
to be defiant and European and — all right, be crushed
by one's environment, but all the same have made
some attempt to remain standing. Of course, this can't
go on indefinitely and in the end I'm bound to lose —
if only at the point where my ashes are immersed in
the Ganges to the accompaniment of Vedic hymns,
and then who will say that I have not truly merged
with India?

I do sometimes go back to Europe. But after a
time I get bored there and want to come back here.
I also find it hard now to stand the European climate.
I have got used to intense heat and seem to need it.

*   *   *

A Bad Woman

It was a tiny house in an outer suburb of Bombay. There was a tiny garden in front and then a porch leading to a passage from which opened two rooms, one on the left and one on the right; the passage ended in a tiny courtyard and the courtyard in a tiny kitchen; that was all. Chameli had been enchanted with the place when he had first brought her there. She thought she would be very happy there (actually, she could be happy anywhere, she had that sort of temperament). She kept everything bright and clean, grew flowers, kept a nightingale in a cage, sewed curtains on a little sewing-machine Sethji had brought for her, and sang all the time. That was during the first few weeks; after that she became a little melancholy.

It was being so alone. She didn't mind being by herself in the house when Sethji had gone back to Delhi; she wasn't afraid, not even in the nights. But it was having no one at all to talk to — no friendly faces around her, no friendly neighbours — that was so depressing. Even during the worst time of her life (the two years of her marriage), she had always had friends and neighbours to gossip and giggle with, so that she had managed to snatch some lighthearted moments in the midst of all her sufferings. But here the people living around her were very unfriendly. Sometimes, true, one or two of the women might drop in on her, and although she was always pleased when they did so, she noticed that they did not come

in a nice neighbourly spirit; she couldn't quite explain
it to herself, but somehow it was almost as if they
had come to spy on her, they looked round them so
carefully and asked her pointed questions and exchanged looks with one another. And if she invited them to
sit down and have something, they either refused or,
if they accepted, sat on the very edge of the chair as
if they were afraid of getting themselves dirty and
tasted anything she gave them in a slow, experimental
way, taking tiny sips or bites and then looking up into
the air as if they were waiting for something bad to
happen to them.

But even if they had been willing to be friendly
with her, she would never have been able to gossip
with them the way she had done with her Delhi
neighbours. There, in Delhi, they had all spoken the
same kind of Hindi : courtly, often oblique, shot
through with little coquetries and pleasantries which
were implicit in the language itself. But here they
spoke mainly Gujerati or Marathi, neither of which
Chameli could understand, and whatever Hindi they
knew was so crude, so lacking in all those refine-
ments which in Delhi came natural as the movements
of the tongue, that it made her wince to have to
listen to it. Her servant, a sour skinny middle-aged
woman called Gangubai, did not speak any Hindi
— or, if she did, pretended not to, so that there was
no communication between them at all, apart from
the contemptuous grunts Gangubai let out in her
mistress' direction from time to time during the course
of her work and unfailingly when it was finished and
she was ready to go home, thrusting her feet back
into the cast-off shoes which had been waiting for her

outside the kitchen door.

Chameli wrote letters to Sethji in Delhi : "When will you come to me? I look out of the window and wait for you. The hours pass slowly. Please bring some Delhi halwa. Please come." There was no answer, so she wrote more letters and the reply came : "Business is urgent here, when it is less pressing I will start. The heat is great and the mango crop has failed, price of mangoes Rs.4 a dozen, no one can afford. It is better if you don't write any more. I am well and happy." So she stopped writing and waited. She paced around the tiny house, and sometimes she rocked herself on the rocking-chair on the porch and looked out with sad eyes at the people passing who often did not greet her, even those who had been to visit her. Three times a day she turned on the radio to listen to her favourite programme of music from the films, and she poked her finger through the bars of her nightingale's cage and talked to it because there was no one else.

Then Sethji came, and she talked and talked and talked and didn't stop, and she ran backwards and forwards serving him, cooking for him, massaging him, doing everything she possibly could think of for him, talking all the time even though she knew he wasn't listening much, till he fell asleep and then she sat by him and fanned her hand over him to keep the flies away. He took his teeth out when he slept, his mouth was open, snores came out of it, and his big jowls quivered. She looked at him and, in spite of herself, she sighed. A tear came out of her eye and splashed on to his cheek; she wiped it away with her hand and when she did so, her fingers lingering over his soft

loose flesh, more tears came, more and more, raining
out of her eyes.

But when he left her to go home to Delhi, she
thought her heart would break. She wanted to cry
out to him, take me with you! to fall at his feet and
implore him. But she didn't. Instead she kept quite
still, didn't say one word, held her face averted so
that he wouldn't be able to see the expression on it.
She knew how impossible it was for him to take her
back to Delhi, where all his family was and everyone
knew him and he was a big man; and how grateful
she ought to be to him for bringing her here to Bombay,
keeping her and hiring this pretty house for her and
a servant to go with it. And she *was* grateful — without
him where would she be? how would she eat? That
was why she kept silent and didn't utter one word
of complaint as she watched him leave. He was very
cheerful, hummed a little tune and pinched her breast
behind the door before waddling down the garden
path in his clean white dhoti, his umbrella in one
hand and the little bundle of provisions she had
prepared for his journey in the other. She watched
his taxi drive away, and it was only when it was
quite out of sight and for a few minutes afterwards
to make sure he hadn't forgotten something and
wasn't coming back, that she left the porch and went
into her bedroom, there to lie across her bed and
give vent to her feelings.

She could no longer bear to stay all day in the
house and began to go out for walks by herself. It was
something at least to get ready for these walks, wear
a pretty sari, powder on her face, flowers in her hair,
and walk daintily down the road holding a parasol

over herself to shield her against the sun. She walked down to the sea. The sand got into her sandals and she took them off and walked with them in her hand, up and down the beach. But she didn't enjoy it. It wasn't like walking by the river in Delhi where there was always something interesting going on, even if it was only the buffaloes wallowing in the water or the holy men doing yoga on the bank. The sea was very boring : nothing but waves rolling, one after another, all the time without stop, wave after foolish wave. What for? Nevertheless she came back the next day, and the next, and walked up and down, watching the waves. It was better than sitting in the house, having to hear Gangubai's snorts of contempt and look out at the women passing by on the street and wish they would come in and talk to her, or at least greet her.

It was on the beach that she first met Ravi. It seemed he came there every day; she saw him sitting there for hours and hours on the same spot on the beach, all by himself. He had some books and sometimes he read in them, but most of the time he simply stared out at the sea or lay on his stomach and idly combed mounds of sand together. He seemed as bored as she was. She began to look out for him and, after some time, realised that he had begun to look out for her too, or at least to be aware of her. From then on it was only a matter of time before they came together. That it took as long as it did was more his fault than hers. She had been ready to smile at him for some time, but whenever their eyes had been about to meet, he would at the last moment look away and scowl.

That scowl of his was his most characteristic

expression. He looked on everyone, on everything, on the whole world with displeasure. It took about a week before he stopped scowling at Chameli, another week before he smiled. But then, what radiance there was in that smile, what depths of pleasure and of love. And she smiled back in the same way. Never had she had such feelings for anyone. She was fond of Sethji, true, but he was thirty years older than she was : whereas Ravi was of her own age and when they were not lovers together then they were friends, or brother and sister, or simply accomplices against all the other people in the world who were all old and knew nothing of the feelings that lived in Chameli and Ravi.

Now the house was as it should always have been, alive and gay. The flowers she grew in pots began to bloom, the nightingale to sing; she washed the curtains, polished the furniture, tried out new recipes, rocked herself on the veranda and smiled at all the women who walked by and didn't greet her. She showered presents of cloth on Gangubai who examined them carefully, holding them up to the light and then folding them away for herself with her usual grunt of contempt. Chameli just laughed at her and, when she left at the end of the day, locked the door behind her with a final laugh and then danced back into the house to bathe and dress and scent herself. When it was dark, Ravi came. They rolled around on the bed and played like children before becoming serious like lovers and then they slept and then they ate and then it was dawn and time for Ravi to creep out of the house and run home to his. After he had gone, she stood by the window and smiled to herself, slowly braiding her hair; she felt heavy and tired though postponing the delicious moment before she would sink on to the bed and drop instantly like a stone into a dreamless sleep from which she would only wake when it was afternoon and not so long to wait before he came again.

Ravi was a student, but after he met Chameli, he did no more studying. Not that he had done very much before. The hours she had seen him lounging on the beach were hours in which he was supposed to have been at his classes; but he found them very tedious, and moreover regarded them as useless. He was not interested in passing any examinations, although his family had high hopes for him and wanted him to become something distinguished like a lawyer or a gazetted government officer. Ravi saw nothing pleasing in such a prospect, on the contrary, it disgusted him, both for its own sake and because it was his family who wanted it. It was a principle with him that anything his family might want, he would want the opposite; they for him stood for everything that was bad in a world which, in any case, was rotten to the core. Chameli was shocked by this attitude of his towards his family. She had always been very fond of her own family, her mother and her father and everyone, and still often shed tears because she could not longer go to them. He laughed at her — "what have they ever done for you?" he asked her. This seemed a strange question to her because the answer to it was so obvious : they had brought her into this world, had looked after her and fed her when she was small and helpless and could not fend for herself. She loved and honoured them for that. What came after was not their fault — who was to know that her husband would turn out the way he did? Her mother too had cried bitterly over her daughter's misfortune, but what could she do? What could anyone do? It was fate. "And now?" Ravi asked her, fiercely, "where are they now?" She stroked his angry face. How childish he was, how little he knew of life and the world. He pushed her hand away and demanded an answer : as if there was an answer anyone could give outright like that in words. He gripped her arms and shook her : "Now you're a bad woman, so they're too good to know you, is that it? Is it? Is it?" His fingers dug deep into her flesh so that tears sprang into her eyes and she cried out in pain. The moment she did so, he gathered her close into his arms, as close as he could, muttering through clenched teeth, "You're mine, mine, mine," and now there were tears in his eyes too.

But though she avoided the subject of her own family, she often returned to talking to him about his. She felt she would have failed in her duty if she did not try to inspire him with some affection for those who had given him birth and to whom sub-sequently he owed everything. But it was a hopeless task. The moment his family was mentioned, his usual scowl spread over his handsome face, he became bitter, and said "You don't know them." If she continued to urge him, then he would burst out into such words of hatred that she had to cover his mouth with her hand fearing that something bad might happen to him for speaking in this way. Afterwards he would feel slightly ashamed, he would turn his face away and mutter "Well they are like that, what can I do," in sulky self-defence.

But from what she pieced together about his family, she couldn't see what it was about them that made him so dislike them. His father was a very rich man, a textile manufacturer with a cloth mill in Bombay and another one in Ahmedabad, whose time and thoughts were concentrated solely — as Ravi said contemptuously — on making more money. But why not? There was nothing to be contemptuous about. It was like that in business, one had to make money, otherwise what was the use of being in business. Chameli thought wistfully of her own father, who had not been in business, but had only a small salary from his job as railway inspector on which they had all had to live. But Ravi said he hated money because it made people greedy and unscrupulous the way his father was and all his uncles. As for his mother and his aunts and all his other female relations, they thought of nothing but the jewellery with which their safes were crammed and which were taken out on big occasions and hung about their persons to dazzle and awe those less well endowed; and in between conferring with their jewellers, or ordering new saris to be embroidered for them, or haggling with the Kashmiri shawl-seller, they spent their time planning advantageous marriages for their children — marriages in which not the happiness of the main protagonists was considered, oh no, that was of no account whatever, but only the question of how much money would be coming into the family, what status they would enjoy in the community, and how grand the wedding festivities were going to be.

Chameli laughed : everything he was saying, with such disgust, was so natural, more, even beautiful and

right, it was what everyone cared for. Everyone liked
to be rich, everyone wanted grand marriages in the
family; and every woman loved jewellery and costly
saris, what did he know about it. Would you like me,
she challenged him, if I didn't wear pretty clothes and
took good care of myself and put on my gold earrings
and bangles? Yes, he said, best of all I like you with
nothing on at all. Oh be quiet, keep your silly mouth
shut, will you — and she gave him a playful slap
which he returned, and after that they were too busy
with one another to talk any more on that subject.

But she came back to it, quite often, even at the
risk of making him scowl. She wanted to educate him
in the ways of the world, of which he was as ignorant
as a child. His notions were, it seemed to her, completely divorced from anything real. She asked him —
all right, so you don't like money, you don't like
your studies, you don't want to be a lawyer or a
gazetted officer, you don't want to marry a rich girl
whom your family will find for you, all right : but
what do you want, what is it? He had no answer, only
some vague ideas which he couldn't put properly into
words, and some lines of poetry about the stars, and
the sea, and the soul. It made her smile. Yes, she too
loved poetry, she loved music, every day she listened
with rapture to songs on the radio that spoke of moonlight and the scent of flowers. But that wasn't life as
one had to live it. It was only the moments snatched
in between, in the teeth of reality, gaiety plucked with
desperate courage out of one's surrounding circumstances. When her husband had turned out to be cruel,
had beaten her and forbidden her to visit or write to
her family, and finally had turned out to have another

wife and three children all of whom he brought to live in the house : at that time whatsoever smiles she could muster, the flashes of happiness that came and went, were just a moment's light relief, a sudden spatter of cool rain-drops scorched up almost at once in the surrounding waste of heat. But what could he know about that? He had suffered so little that he thought it was these flashes that were real and could be for ever. She tousled his hair, she kissed his neck; she loved his innocence, but she feared for him too, for his awakening.

She feared most at present what would happen when Sethji came again. She had worked out a signal for Ravi : when Sethji came, she would replace the usual light bulb on the porch with a green one, and as long as the green bulb was there, Ravi must stay away. She kept impressing this on him, and he made no comment beyond a gloomy assent. "It won't be for long," she comforted him. "He never stays long." She scanned his face anxiously — his young, young beautiful face — but he turned it away from her, rolled over on to his stomach, buried his head under a pillow and, it seemed, went to sleep.

Unexpected, unannounced, so that she was glad she had the green bulb all ready, Sethji came. It was not difficult for her to pretend she was happy to see him. In a way, she *was* happy : she liked Sethji, she was grateful to him, she knew how much she owed him. And of course he brought news from home — not of her family, true, he had no contact with them, but at least of the streets, the shops, the weather. She plied him with questions — is the new cinema in Patel Nagar ready yet? were there many dust storms? did the rains come on time? — so many, that he threw up his hands and laughed and begged for time to answer. Then she asked, looking away from him, ashamed, drawing circles with her forefinger, how is Bibiji and all of them? And Sethji too turned his face away and said yes, they were well, all well. Bibiji and all of them were his wife and family, to whom Chameli was truly attached and who had been so kind to her. It was they who had taken her in when she had run away from her husband, and her own father and mother had not allowed her to come home again. In her desperation she had run to Bibiji's house — who had been kind to her in the past, had bought some of her embroideries and commissioned more — and Bibiji had taken her in, had allowed her to live with them and do sewing work and other tasks around the house. If it had not been for Bibiji, what would have happened to Chameli? That was why she was ashamed when she thought of her, because she owed her so much. Probably Bibiji hated her now and had very bad thoughts about her, and of course she was right. But if it had not been Chameli, it might have been someone else, someone who would have demanded a lot of money and made trouble and not been content, like Chameli, to be taken hundreds of miles away to Bombay and left there.

She cooked for Sethji with the same care as she did for Ravi, and tendered to all his needs with true devotion. He was pleased with her — patted her in various places and pinched her and said with approval that she was getting fat, Bombay seemed to suit her. And Chameli laughed out loud with pleasure, because she felt that yes, Bombay did suit her. Her body had attained a sort of joyful ripeness, and she liked passing her hands downwards from her breasts over her stomach and hips to feel herself burgeoning, her young flesh swelling. Her arms in particular were very plump and shapely, and how graceful they looked coming out of the short sleeves and adorned with many bangles. She was, moreover, bubbling over with good spirits, ran here and there to lavish a hundred little attentions on Sethji, light on her feet in spite of her heavy burden of breasts and hips, and exquisite as a courtesan in all her movements; when he had finished eating, she sat on the floor in front of him and, pressing his calves and ankles with skilful fingers, she sang a tender love-song which, even though her voice was untrained, was full of sweet, true feeling. Sethji sighed with contentment and soon he was asleep on the bed, with his head sunk deep in the soft pillows.

She stayed lying beside him for a while, and then she got up and quietly, on naked feet, crept outside on to the porch. She stood under the green bulb and peered out into the street. But it was silent and empty; there was no one there. The night was warm and very still, and the houses opposite, usually full of noise and activity, looked frozen in moonlight. She waited under the green bulb, full of longing, her heart so strained with yearning that surely he must feel it. But he did not come, and at last, after waiting for a long time, she gave up, went back inside, and lay down next to Sethji.

This was repeated every night. As soon as Sethji was asleep, she would creep out and wait on the porch. And wait, night after night, in vain. She looked forward impatiently to Sethji's departure and, when the day

C

finally came, she joyfully watched him walking off
down the little garden path, carrying his umbrella and
his food parcel tied up in a cloth. She could hardly
wait for the taxi to turn the corner, and at once went
inside to fetch a chair. She stood on it, on tiptoe, and
stretched up to unscrew the green bulb. Gangubai
watched her suspiciously. Chameli gave her the bulb
as a present, and then she took a beautiful piece of
sky-blue satin out of her trunk and gave her that
as well.

Later that night, when Gangubai had gone home,
Chameli sat by the window, bathed, powdered, scented, wearing her prettiest sari of all, every nail brightly
polished, henna on the soles of her feet and the palms
of her hands and in the parting of her hair. A rich
jasmine scent rose from her body and from sticks of
incense which she had lighted all round the house.
Everything was ready for him and she sat and waited
and looked impatiently at the clock. But that night
too he did not come. She went out and paced impatiently on the porch. The sleep and silence all
around her nearly drove her mad. She wanted to shout
out loud "Where are you?" It was as if she was alone
in the world. She went back into the house and
suddenly began to claw at her hair which she had
taken so much trouble to arrange. One earring came
undone and rolled under the bed and she crawled
along the floor to look for it. But she gave up quite
soon and simply stayed lying on the floor. Once she
raised her head and gave out one long, loud cry. She
thought perhaps she would never see him again and
she could not bear it.

But she did see him again, the very next day. She

went out to look for him and found him on the
beach, in the same spot as she had seen him in the
beginning, and in the same way, his books disregarded
by his side, lying on his stomach and idly combing
sand together. She sat down beside him and, without
looking up, he said at once "Go away." She took no
notice but moved a little closer : to see him again,
be near him, was all she wanted. She didn't want to
reproach him even for causing her such suffering. That
was finished now and they were together again.

"Don't come near me," he said.

She smiled and put out her hand to touch his hair;
even when he jerked away from her, she still continued
to smile. He looked so charming when he was being
sulky : his eyes were lowered and his long lashes
quivered on his cheeks. He was as beautiful as a girl,
and yet already there was such manliness in him, a
promise of such strength.

"Listen," she said. "It's not my fault. What can I
do? I have to live, and he's kind to me. That's all. Like
a father."

He groaned and buried his face in his arms, lying
flat on his stomach in the sand.

"When you are older it will be different. Then you
will take care of me." She spoke to him soothingly
in words that didn't mean much. She couldn't think
of him as older, and certainly it had never occurred to
her that he would take care of her, the way Sethji did
now. And anyway, the future was not important to
her, and she spoke only to make him feel better.

He sat up, but he still didn't look at her. He scooped
up fistfuls of sand from between his feet and watched
it trickling from out of his fingers. He appeared not to

be listening to her, but she knew that he was. She had moved closer to him and was speaking to him very intimately, in a low voice. They were almost alone on the whole wide beach. People did not come here in the mornings, and there were only one or two coconut-sellers who had nowhere else to go, and a few boys, a long way off at the sea's edge, picking up jelly-fish and shells. Chameli no longer spoke of the future but of the past. She recalled to him all the things they had done together, and the account was thrilling, and thrilling the way she told it. "Remember?" she kept saying, close to his ear, and gently touched him with one finger, and though he didn't answer, she saw his mouth-corner twitch. And at last, with one particularly telling little occurrence she recalled to his memory, she won him over completely, so that he left off sifting sand and, flinging himself down in abandon, burst into a loud roar of laughter. She too laughed, but in a refined, coy manner, turning her head aside and covering her mouth with her hand; and she wished that they were at home now, the two of them, in the dark room on the bed on which they did all the things of which she had spoken, instead of out here in the glaring light of day amid dull, empty wastes of sand and sea.

He began to come again night after night. But something had changed, they were no longer as happy as they had been. Chameli did her best — made herself pretty, cooked lovely meals — but the old times did not come back again. It was almost as if Ravi didn't want them back again. He was abrupt with her, often rude, rejecting all her little tendernesses. Nor did he now confide his feelings to her the way he had done before when he had talked about the stars, and the sky, and the soul, and if she mentioned his family, he replied with a shrug as if they no longer bothered him. Nothing any longer bothered him. He seemed vacant and like one who did not care what happened to him. He often smelled of drink, and she began to suspect that he visited the little huts in the creeks where illicit liquor was distilled and which were frequented by bad characters. But when she asked him, he made no reply and, if she insisted, he turned on her so fiercely that she was afraid and had to keep quiet.

There was something reckless and violent about him now which had not been there before. He often hurt her and, if she cried out, he laughed and did it again. He had become skilled and self-confident, and all that boyish awkwardness which she had so adored had gone. And after he had finished making love, he no longer sank into an innocent sleep as he used to do, but he would get up, wearing only a lungi, his chest naked, and swagger restlessly around the house. He was ravenously hungry, and though she always served him a meal soon after he came, towards midnight or the early hours of the morning he would ask for more food and, when she gave it to him, he sat on the floor and gulped it down greedily. Once, as she watched him eating thus, he suddenly reminded her of her husband, who had always eaten in the same greedy way : so that she cried out "Don't!" and Ravi looked up and his eyes stared straight into hers, and at that moment they too reminded her of her husband, for they were no longer the brooding, dreaming eyes that she had known but, as if a veil had been torn from them, stark, bold, manly, cruel.

Often he didn't want to leave. He might be lying on the bed when it was time to go, heavily asleep after the big meal he had eaten, and when she tried to shake him awake, he would grunt and mutter to be left alone. She begged, she pleaded, finally in her desperation she threw cold water over him, drenching him and the bed. He sat up, cursed her, shook himself like a dog, while she hurriedly helped him to dress and, almost dragging him off the bed, thrust him towards the door and out into the street. By that time it was almost dawn, and she was terrified that he would be seen, by the milkman and the newspaper boys and the first early morning walkers, as he made his way to his own house, still wet, still half asleep, and staggering like a drunkard.

He had become so reckless that once he even came in the day, when Gangubai was still there. Chameli was sewing herself a new blouse on her little sewing-machine, and she was just inserting the cloth under the needle when she heard his voice calling her from outside. She gave a start and the needle went deep into her finger so that the blood came spurting out. Thrusting it into her mouth to suck up the blood, she went running out and found him standing right there on the verandah for all the world to see. She pulled him inside, into the little passage, and then pushed him into the bedroom and bolted the door. He smelled strongly of liquor and was swaying a bit.

"Why have you come?" she whispered.

"To sleep," he replied and sank promptly on to the bed. She shook him to make him get up again : "Go away, go quickly," she said in a low voice, hoping

Gangubai would not hear. But already Gangubai was pounding on the door, shouting : "Did you call me?"

"No no!" Chameli shouted back. "Let me alone! I'm resting!"

"Who is that?" Ravi asked, and Gangubai demanded from outside the door : "Has anyone come?"

"No one!" Chameli cried in agony. She put her hand over Ravi's mouth and called to Gangubai "Go away! Do your work!" as peremptorily as she could. She heard the servant muttering to herself and waited to hear her move away, out into the courtyard. Only then did she take her hand from Ravi's mouth.

"What's the matter?" he asked; he was already half asleep. Suddenly she noticed that his face was smeared with blood. She wondered whether he had been in a fight, but a moment later realised that the blood came from her own finger, which was still bleeding. She tore two strips from the end of her sari; one of them she tied impatiently round her finger, the other she dipped into water and began to wash her blood from Ravi's face. She did this tenderly, lovingly, like a mother to her child, kneeling on the floor by the bed and gazing down into his sleeping face. But what she saw there frightened her. She recalled his face as she had first known it — sulky but soft, rounded, misty, full of boyish innocence; now all that had gone. What had happened? What had changed him so quickly? She felt bewildered and sad.

From that day on the stream of presents given to Gangubai never stopped : now it was not only lengths of cloth, but money too, and once or twice pieces of jewellery. Gangubai received everything without comment, without change of expression; she had even given up her previous snorts of contempt but was now only a silent, passive figure around the house, arriving punctually at the same hour every morning, leaving punctually at the same hour every evening. She was clean and scrupulous in her work and beyond reproach. But Gangubai was not Chameli's only worry. The neighbouring women had begun to interest themselves in her again, and sometimes when she looked out of the window she saw a little group of them gathered outside, their heads close together, whispering excitedly and every now and again throwing looks over their shoulders towards the house. If she sat on the porch, some of them would stop to greet her and even linger a bit as if they wanted to say something more or hoped to be asked in. One or two of the bolder ones did come in, without being asked, they sat in her house and looked around them with glittering eyes, and once she even caught them bending down to peer under the sofa as if they suspected she was hiding someone there.

She lived, day and night, in fear. Fear of Ravi himself, of what he would do next, the violence that seemed to be smouldering in him, the recklessness; and of the consequences of that recklessness, which already had awakened suspicion and hostility all around her. Any day now she feared his family would take action against her, and she had visions of them in their big white house (the men weighty and rich, the women in gorgeous saris and bedecked with jewellery) deciding to call in the police to have her turned out of her house and thrown into jail or confined in one of those homes for fallen women where she would have to wear thick white cotton saris and be taught to spin. She started at every noise — thinking, they have come, they are here — and no longer dared to sit in the porch and indeed, after a while, to leave her bedroom. She kept herself locked in there, wouldn't let Gangubai come in to clean, no longer bothered to bathe and dress herself. Her nightingale, left alone in its cage, ceased to sing, her flowers, which she neglected to water, withered and died. She sat all day, played patience with herself, peered from behind the curtain, and cried from fear and despair.

Ravi continued, night after night, to visit her. He never missed, though often she longed for him not to come. But if he was even a little late, she began to pace up and down the room wondering what had happened, whether his family had locked him up or whether he had got into trouble in one of those little huts in which he now spent so much of his time drinking illicit liquor. When at last he came, her relief was always tempered with annoyance, and she frequently thought to herself, if only he would leave me alone, just for one night. Sometimes she begged him to do so — she said she wasn't well, needed rest — but he never heeded her and came all the same. She no longer bothered to take any trouble for him — often she didn't even change her sari or comb her hair, and the food she served him was badly cooked and mostly stale. He appeared not to care, or even to notice, Sometimes he hardly talked to or looked at her at all, he simply ate and went to sleep, and later woke her up to give him something more to eat. But once, just once, it was as it had been before and they loved each other with the same fervour as at the beginning. That night all that had happened in between, all the changes they had undergone, dropped away and they slept in each other's arms like children and both cried with relief and happiness and then they laughed and, drop by drop, kissed each other's tears away. So the next night she waited for him eagerly, all spruced up again in a pink silk sari with little silver stars on it, but when he came, he was drunk and, in answer to her remonstrances, hit her on the face and made her nose bleed.

After all that how great was her relief when, one fine day, Sethji came back again! She gaily climbed on to a chair and put a new green bulb in and, that done, danced back into the house to devote herself entirely to him. She could hardly bear to take her eyes away from him : she loved to see him sitting there in her house, comfortable, solid, round all over from the round little bald patch on his head down to his round belly and his short round feet. He laughed at the fuss she made of him, but laughed with pleasure, and soon he took his teeth out, as always when he felt very comfortable, so that his face fell into kind old lines and when he laughed he showed his empty gums like a sweet harmless old baby. She sat at his feet and massaged his legs slowly and tenderly and, while she was doing this, she looked up at him with adoring eyes. He patted her cheek and said "What's the matter? You look pulled down;" she said "That's because I've been waiting for you so long;" she shut her eyes passionately, murmuring "Waiting and waiting and waiting and waiting," and then, though he tried to prevent her, she crouched down to lay her head in a gesture of submission and devotion on his feet.

But later at night, when he was asleep, she got up again from his side and crept out on to the porch.

She was afraid of whom she would find there : yet, though she had been half expecting him, she could not suppress a little cry when she actually saw him. Lit up by the green bulb, he was leaning against the balustrade of the porch, looking silently towards the house. He didn't say anything to her, neither did he move.

She clutched him by both arms and whispered "Please go."

"What harm am I doing?"

"No," she kept saying; "no." She pulled at his arms and he allowed himself to be dragged out into the street, quite docilely; he seemed sad rather than anything else. And seeing him like that, she too became sad. She pleaded with him "What can I do? Is it my fault." Suddenly they embraced and clung to each other, in the middle of the empty street in front of all those silent, sleeping houses. They didn't say anything to each other, but they stayed like that for some time. At last she freed herself from him and said "You go first," and she watched him walking away, and then she went back indoors to lie again by Sethji's side.

Later she woke up with a start. She sat up in bed and listened, but there was no sound; she tiptoed quietly out on to the porch but it was empty. Nevertheless her heart continued to pound with fear — till at last she could stand it no longer. She shook Sethji by the shoulder and said into his sleeping ear "Please take me away from here."

He did not wake up easily, and even when he did, partly heaving himself out of the depths of middle-aged sleep, he thought she was talking in her dreams

and made clucking noises at her. But she shook him
again by the shoulder and said "Put me anywhere you
like, only take me away from here."

He was bewildered, not understanding what it was
all about in the middle of the night, so she began to
make up reasons for him: the Bombay climate did not
suit her, she was lonely, she had no friends, she didn't
care for the food, her servant stole from her —
desperately she made up one thing after another, and
at last burst into sobs and beat her hands against his
chest, crying like a child "Take me away, take me
away!"

He attempted to soothe her, promised that they
would talk about it in the morning, he would see to
everything, make it all well, till at last she lay down
again and allowed him to go back to sleep. She herself
continued to be awake, lying on her back, her eyes
wide open, listening, waiting.

She did not have to wait long. She heard his foot-
steps running along the road, then up the path to
her house, and next moment he was pounding on the
outer door. She ran to open it before the noise could
waken Sethji. Ravi pushed past her without even
looking at her. He strode into the bedroom and turned
on the light and looked at Sethji lying there. Sethji
sat up in bed; his hand went to his heart, he cried
"Who is it? What?" He looked old and afraid and his
toothless mouth had dropped open.

Chameli tried to hold on to Ravi, but Ravi was a
big strong man now. He advanced towards the bed
and he pushed Sethji down. Chameli heard bleating
sounds from Sethji, and she saw Ravi's face swelling
and turning dark with fury and effort as he strained

and strained, with his hands round Sethji's neck. Chameli ran away. Right out of the house, along all the streets, till she got to the beach and to the sea and could get no further. She sank down at the edge of the sea where the waves rolled as endlessly, as boringly as ever. But she didn't mind them now — on the contrary, she asked for nothing better than to be allowed to sit here in peace and watch them.

*   *   *

A Star and Two Girls

No one knew who had brought the two English girls to the party. It was the usual kind of film star's party, with a lot of illicit liquor and heavy Indian food; and the usual kind of people were there, like directors and playback singers and actors and lots of hangers-on. It was the hangers-on who got drunk the quickest, and one of them had to be carried out quite early. There were also some well-known actresses, and they all wore plain white saris and no jewellery and sat very demurely with their eyes cast down so that it was evident at one glance that they were virtuous. The two English girls, on the other hand, were not a bit demure but looked around them with bright eyes and were ready to talk to anyone who talked to them. Their names were Gwen and Maggie.

Suraj, who gave the party in honour of his own birthday, had good reason to be satisfied with it. It went on till four o'clock in the morning, most people were drunk and some so drunk that they got sick; a lot of jokes were told which the actresses had to pretend not to understand. At the height of good spirits several men broke into a rough, spontaneous dance, while the others stood round in a circle and rhythmically clapped and cheered them on to dance more and more wildly till they collapsed in exhaustion on the floor, and then everyone laughed and helped them to their feet again. An excellent party in every way, and next day, lying in bed at noon, Suraj thought back on it with satisfaction. However, he found that what he thought most about was the two English girls, and here his satisfaction was not entirely unmixed. Although friendly, there had been something aloof about them, and Suraj even had a hazy memory — all memories of the party were hazy for he had drunk a good deal — of some kind of a rebuff. What had happened? What was it? He couldn't remember, he only had a vague idea that his advances — not even advances, his friendliness — were not met with the same eager gratitude that he was used to. And then quite suddenly, quite early too, the two girls had left. One minute they were there, and the next, just as he turned round to look for them again, they had gone. He frowned, then laughed. He was going to find them again; for nothing in particular, only for his own amusement. It was something to look forward to.

Gwen and Maggie were pleased to see him when he turned up at their hotel. Indeed, anyone would have been pleased to see Suraj : he was tremendously hand-some and wore beautiful clothes and walked in the way people do who know everyone is looking at them. He had real star quality. Gwen and Maggie were not, however, absolutely bowled over by this; they kept their heads and this pleased Suraj and at the same time put him on his mettle. He wanted very much to have them like and admire him and found himself eager to do a great deal for them. He wanted to introduce them to the film world, to show them Bombay, to throw everything open for them. He escorted them to expensive restaurants and took them for long drives in his car. He invited them to his shooting sessions and showed them round the studios and introduced them to many famous stars. He was

eager for them to pronounce an impossible wish so
that he might be able to fulfil it. But all their wishes
were quite possible and the most he could do was to
fulfil them to the brim, doing everything on as large
and grand a scale as possible. He took them to the
races, and a polo match, and a wrestling bout, and a
cricket match, and everywhere they had front seats
and were made much of because they were with him.
They accepted all this gladly and were always profuse
in words of appreciation and gratitude. "It was quite
perfect," they would say. "Thank you so much for
taking us." "Tremendous . . . fabulous . . . thanks
most awfully . . . absolutely marvellous": but he
sensed that it was only their words that were so profuse,
and that actually they were not as overwhelmed as
they pretended to be. On the contrary, he felt there
was something detached and amused in their attitude,
and indeed they took everything so much in their
stride that he became quite frantic in trying to think
up more and more, better and better treats for them.
Sometimes he was annoyed at their levelheadedness,
and then annoyed at himself that he — he, Suraj! —
should care to impress them.

He always thought of them together : Gwen and
Maggie, as if they were one person. Yet they were very
different. Maggie was large, pretty, ash-blonde, with a
radiant smile and dimples in her healthy cheeks; Gwen,
on the other hand, didn't look a bit healthy — in
fact, she looked rather consumptive or at least as if
she had a weak chest, very thin and with a deathly
pale, transparent skin and light red hair. They had
been at school together and had all sorts of jokes from
that time which Suraj didn't understand; now they

were on a world trip which their parents had given them as a present on their eighteenth birthdays. When they got back, Maggie hoped to start work on a fashion magazine, Gwen had been promised a job in an art gallery. Neither of them was in a hurry to return home, though, and start on this new life.

What they liked to do best was to lie for hours and hours on the beach. Gwen would shelter herself under a parasol because her skin was so delicate, but Maggie would lie in full sunshine wearing a tight, bright yellow swimming-costume and smeared with suntan oil, lying now on her back and now on her stomach so that both sides should get done equally. Suraj would get restless and ask "What shall we do now?" but they wouldn't even answer him, they were so drowsy and content. Sometimes Maggie went off into the sea with him, and there she shrieked and kicked her arms and legs and fought with him among the waves, while Gwen watched them from under her parasol, looking composed and rather elegant in some sort of flowing, flowered shift. When they came back again, Suraj rubbed a towel vigorously to and fro across his back but Maggie simply flopped down on the sand and let the sun dry the drops of water from her skin.

"Aren't you hungry?" Suraj asked hopefully. He himself was starving — he always needed a lot of food at regular times and his swim in the sea combined with the idle morning had left him hungrier than ever. But those two, if they bothered to answer him at all, only shook their heads; it wasn't as if they didn't have hearty appetites — they did, whenever they settled down to a meal, he was amazed at the quantities they put away with unabashed relish — but only that they

D

couldn't be bothered to move. "It's restful here," Gwen murmured, and Maggie, lying face down on the sand, said "Hmm" in luxurious assent. Suraj was afraid they would drop off to sleep, and then he would patiently have to wait till they woke up before he could get anything to eat, so he began to talk rather desperately, using a loud, wide-awake voice to rouse them :

"Yesterday we saw my new rushes. Everyone said they are wonderful, this is going to be a big hit. Everyone said."

"What fun."

"They said it is my best role yet. I play a poor rickshaw-wallah and one day my sister is abducted by a rich man. The scene in which I realise what has happened is very emotional. There is no dialogue, only the expression on my face. It was a great strain playing this scene — ooph, afterwards I felt exhausted, terrible. You don't know what it is like for an actor : you see, we really *feel* what we are acting and it is, oh I can't explain, but a great burden here, here on the heart." He clutched it.

"I know exactly what you mean," Gwen said. "I was in the school play once — you remember, Mag? It was only a small part but it was agony. Of course I muffed the whole thing and was never taken again in any other school play which was disappointing but also a tremendous relief because I honestly don't think I could ever have lived through such moments of fearful dread again."

"Don't be an ass," said Maggie and made amused sounds from out of the sand.

"I'm completely serious," Gwen insisted, and then

she looked at Suraj with wide, green eyes : "She doesn't understand. But you do, don't you? You know what I mean."

He felt uncomfortable. Was she laughing at him? But her eyes, as she looked at him unblinkingly, were clear and frank. He dared not answer but instead laughed to show that he understood the joke (if it was a joke). Then he shouted : "But aren't you hungry yet? Aren't you starving?"

He enjoyed looking at them and beyond that he enjoyed the fact that they liked to be looked at. It was not so with pretty Indian girls — or if it was, they did their best to hide it, putting on a proud, injured air, giving little tosses of the head and twitching at their saris. But Gwen and Maggie bathed in admiration as if it were sunshine, they smiled and basked themselves like cats. When they were on the beach together, Suraj loved feasting his eyes on Maggie's naked thighs as they came bursting — so firm, golden and healthy, brushed with a down of blonde hair and grains of sand — from out of her tight yellow swimming-costume; and far from discouraging him, Maggie kept shifting them from here to there so that he could see them better, and sometimes she looked at them herself, likewise with admiration and approval, and tenderly brushed the sand off them. On the other hand, Suraj got very annoyed if anyone else looked at the two girls. Unfortunately most people did, not only because the two were young and pretty but also because they were foreign and different. Sometimes Suraj made scenes on this score — in restaurants, in cinema foyers, suddenly he would seize someone by the shirt-front and thrust his face forward and say rude, challenging

things in Hindi. The two girls would try and calm
him down and get him away as quickly as possible,
almost hustling him off while he continued to throw
furious glances at the offender and his big strong
shoulders twitched inside the silk shirt, impatient for
a fight.

But the worst scene was with one of his own
friends. Suraj had many friends. They liked to be with
him wherever he went, and he liked to have them
there : they gave each other confidence, he to move
in the middle of a crowd who applauded and, where
possible, imitated his every word and action, they to
be seen and known in the company of a celebrity.
They sat in his house from early morning, eating his
food and drinking his liquor and smoking his cigarettes,
they accompanied him on the set and loudly applauded every shot of his, they thronged to his parties, they
begged for passes to his premieres, they accompanied
him on his travels at his expense. When he wished
them to go away — which was not very often, though
more often than usual now that he had met Gwen and
Maggie — he told them so quite without ceremony;
and indeed they did not expect ceremony from him.
He would not allow them to see much of the two
English girls. He knew only too well what thoughts
they would have, what ribald comments they would
pass about them to each other — he had often enough
made the same kind of comments himself. But now
the idea made him angry. The girls were his friends,
they were under his protection. His companions realised his feelings, so that when they did meet the girls,
which was sometimes unavoidable, they were on their
guard and were careful to throw nothing but covert

glances in that direction and to pass their comments
well out of their patron's earshot.

Once, however, one of them spoke too loudly. It
was a very hot and trying day, on the set of one of
Suraj's films. An excellent scene, full of dramatic and
emotional content, had been planned for that day,
and Suraj had invited the two English girls to be
present. However, everything went wrong. The electri-
cians could not fix the lights to the cameraman's
satisfaction and everyone had to sit around and wait,
and then the leading lady's make-up had to be done
again. It was the sort of frustrating day that happened
often enough in Suraj's professional career; but today
it infuriated him because of his two guests whom he
had specially invited to witness one of his great scenes.
He sat and smoked cigarette after cigarette, frowning
and not speaking much, and feeling very hot in his
costume which consisted of silk leggings, a cloth of
gold coat, and a huge silk turban with a jewel and a
feather in it. Everyone was in a bad mood. The
director and the cameraman shouted at each other,
and the assistant director had an argument with the
sound recordist, and the leading lady got angry with
the tailor who kneeled on the floor sewing spangles
on to her Moghul princess dress. Suraj's friends yawned
and were restless and called for many bottles of coca-
cola. Only Gwen and Maggie were not bored. They
sat on the two chairs allotted to them, one in a
raspberry pink dress and the other in a lemon yellow
one, sucking cold drinks through a straw and looking
very happy to be there and grateful that they had
been invited.

The heat, the boredom, the fact that Suraj seemed

to be preoccupied made his friends more careless than usual. They began to point out certain characteristics of the two English girls to each other — for instance, that they happened to be showing a great deal of long leg — and they tittered together and one of them volunteered a remark which was certainly funny but was unfortunately overheard by Suraj. Quick as a flash he jumped up (his chair fell over) and the next thing that was heard was a resounding slap. Those that had been quarrelling or arguing stopped doing so and it was suddenly very quiet in that noisy place so that the next slap sounded even louder than the first. The leading lady let out a little cry of terror. After the second slap, Suraj's victim hid his head in his arms; otherwise he made no attempt to defend himself, nor did he offer to run away but stood as if awaiting any further chastisement his patron might wish to inflict. Suraj began to belabour him with his fists, the feather in his turban shook and trembled furiously as he rained blows on the young man's head and shoulders; since no resistance was offered, he continued to do so until others begged him to desist and hung on to his arms. The leading lady cried "Oh, oh" as she watched, and from time to time she flung her hands before her face as if she could not bear to see any more. Gwen and Maggie averted their eyes from the scene of violence, and when it was over, they sat very quiet, no longer bright and interested and happy to be there but, on the contrary, as if they were uncomfortable and wished to be away.

When next he saw them, Suraj had forgotten about this incident and was surprised when they brought it up. "It's all right," he said, waving his hand to wave it all away. "He has apologised to me."

"*He* apologised to *you!*"

"Yes," Suraj said and stared at them and they stared back at him. There was a brief silence. Then Suraj said "Hurry up, aren't you ready yet?" He had come to the hotel to fetch them and take them out to witness a gala beauty contest.

Gwen said "You know, I think I don't feel like it."

"Me neither," Maggie said. They both took off their shoes and lay down on their twin beds.

"Are you ill?"

"Not ill exactly," Gwen said.

"Our table is booked! Everyone is expecting us!"

"You go, Suraj. Who cares if we're there or not. You're the big attraction."

He paced the room in agitation. He ran his hand through his hair. "What is this? Good heavens. First you say yes, we are coming, and now — "

"I know. We're awful."

He stood by the window. The room, on the third floor of the hotel, overlooked the sea and the curtains were drawn right back, giving a clear view out. Dusk had fallen and the sea looked silver and so did the sky and the ships that lay out on the water. Suraj looked out, and it was so peaceful that his agitation subsided, leaving him instead sad, melancholy. He said "Something is wrong." He turned back into the room and looked at them.

"It's what you did yesterday," Gwen said at once, and Maggie too came in with "It made us feel dreadful." Both seemed relieved to be able to talk about it to him, and they went on in a rush : "It was so unfair, Suraj. That poor boy, after all, what had he done? Nothing."

"Wait," Suraj said.

"To humiliate him like that in front of everyone — how could you? It was so shaming. Unbearable. Oh God, Suraj." And they blushed, their faces red with someone else's shame.

"Wait," Suraj said again. But strangely enough, he was grateful to them for being so frank with him. He remembered the differences he had had with Indian women of his acquaintance — not only with girl friends but with relatives too, with his own mother or sisters. If for some reason they were offended with him, they would be haughty, toss their head, shrug one shoulder, push out their underlip, be eloquent in injured silence; and it was not until he had done a hundred little acts of propitiation that they would at last consent to tell him what he had done to offend them. Gwen and Maggie's directness surprised and pleased him. His feelings towards them grew very warm, and while of course he wanted to acquit himself, he was also at the same time eager to meet their frankness with an even greater one of his own, to explain and to describe his life, his whole world, and make them understand him utterly.

He told them about his own earlier years when he had run away from home and come to Bombay to become a film star. He had been very poor and dependent on other people's goodwill even for food and shelter. Fortunately, he had acquired a patron, a successful film star who had allowed him to join his retinue and follow him around wherever he went. How grateful Suraj had been for this privilege! It had enabled him to penetrate straightaway into that world which he had come to conquer, to pass freely in and

out of studios, be present at story conferences, see
the newest rushes, go to film-world parties, drink the
whisky and smoke the cigarettes which he would never
have been able to afford on his own. In return, all
that his patron required was perfect obedience and
perfect allegiance, to be there when he was feeling
bored or lonely, to laugh at his jokes, to praise him
and run down his rival. All this Suraj and the star's
other friends did gladly, vying with each other as to
who could do it the best; and not only because the
star was who he was, no, but because they genuinely
loved and admired and looked up to him. "He was
like a god to me!" Suraj exclaimed, and his whole
face shone with this past adoration.

Gwen and Maggie, still lying on their beds, smiled
at his fervour. They appreciated it very much. Maggie
said "I wish I could feel like that about someone."

Gwen said "Did you know that in the fourth I was
mad about Miss Kemp? Except I couldn't stand the
way she spat when she spoke."

"Even today," Suraj said, "well — he is not so
great any more, I will tell you, he doesn't get half
the amount, not one quarter, for a film that I get,
and everyone knows he drinks too much and other
vices also. Well, he is old now. But even today, when
I meet him — he can say, Suraj, run out and get me a
packet of cigarettes, and I would run if he ordered
me like that, yes today! Once, years ago, he humiliated
me in front of everyone because he was angry with
me. I felt bad, of course, I went away and cried and
wanted to be dead; but not for one moment did I
feel angry with him — only with myself because I had
offended him. Next day I went back and touched his

feet and begged his pardon and he forgave me. How I loved him at that moment, how grateful I was to him. He was my father, my guide, my guru. I owed everything only to him."

"I'm starving," Maggie suddenly said.

Suraj jumped up and said "Let's go out! Let me take you to — " He racked his brains for somewhere glorious and wonderful enough where he could spend a lot of money and make them happy.

But they preferred to stay in the hotel. They rang the bell and a lot of food was ordered and brought up. They all three ate heartily and sent for several more dishes so that the room became cluttered with used plates and silver dishcovers. Afterwards they leaned out of the window and looked at the sea and the strings of light on the shore and those on the ships far out on the water, and they threw out bread crumbs for the seagulls though these were all asleep. They competed as to who could throw them the furthest, and Suraj won hands down and that made him happier than ever — he loved winning games; and he thought, leaning out of the window between them both, that never in all his life had he enjoyed such a grand friendship, such jolly times as he had with these two English girls.

Yet there were occasions when he was annoyed with them. Suddenly he would suspect that they didn't take him seriously enough; that they didn't realise quite who he was. Then he felt compelled to tell them. Last year he had been voted Actor of the Year by the All India Critics Association; he had more than five hundred fan letters every day; all over the country there were Suraj Fan Clubs who wore badges and celebrated his birthday and organised teas at which to meet each other and talk about him. Gwen and Maggie listened to him politely and made their usual appreciative remarks of "How fascinating" or "How lovely" or "What fun." It wasn't enough : he couldn't quite say what more it was he wanted from them but only that he wanted more, much more, he wanted them to get excited and look at him the way other girls did. And because they didn't do that, they didn't lose their heads, he went and lost his : he became very boastful and told them not only of the grand things he had done and was doing but the even grander ones that lay waiting for him in the future. They continued to listen politely though they no longer commented, and their silence made him talk louder and bigger, his claims became exaggerated and ridiculous, and the worst of it was that he himself was aware of this and was ashamed of it: but instead of keeping quiet, he felt compelled to talk more and more, even thrusting out his chest and beating the flat of his hand against it, at the same time hating himself, and hating them for bringing him to this pass.

On the next day he lay in bed and thought resentful thoughts about them. They were really nothing more than two very ordinary English girls of whom he himself had seen plenty; there was absolutely no reason why they should have so high an opinion of themselves. He decided that he hated people who had a high opinion of themselves. He also decided that he would not see them any more. He stayed in bed and had his breakfast and then his friends came and sat round the bed and they all played cards and had a lot of jokes. It was good fun. Later in the day he sent

them away and got dressed very nicely and went to
visit an actress friend. He was pleased with the
reception he got there. She fussed over him and so
did her mother and they pampered him with a rich
tea of fritters and sweetmeats. He sat with them in
their drawingroom which was rather dark but had lots
of furniture and ornaments and red velvet curtains.
There was teasing and tittering and the actress sat
with her hands demurely in her lap and her eyelids
lowered except sometimes when she raised them a
tiny bit to dart a look of fire at him. A crumb of
sweetmeat had got enticingly stuck to her lip and,
when her mother left the room for a moment, he
darted forward to kiss it away while she tried to ward
him off with her soft, weak arms. Then some photographers came to take her publicity pictures, and
although Suraj wanted her to send them away, she
wouldn't but posed for them in various attitudes in
her drawingroom. Now she looked reflective by a vase
of flowers and holding one flower in her hand, now
she stuck her finger through the bars of her parrot's
cage and tenderly puckered her mouth at him, now
she was gay and threw back her head and laughed
with spontaneous laughter into the cameras. All the
time she was very sweet with the photographers,
dazzling them with charm, while Suraj watched and
got more and more cross. When they had gone, he
began to pick a quarrel with her to which she was
not slow to respond, and soon they were taunting each
other with their shortcomings in both their personal
and professional lives. The mother, after attempting
to soothe them down, joined in on the daughter's
side, but before the quarrel could reach its climax,

Suraj got up in disgust and left them. Surprised and disappointed, they called after him "What's the matter? Why are you going?" but he didn't bother to answer. When he got home, there was a telephone message from the actress, and she kept trying to ring him the whole evening till in the end he took the receiver off the hook.

He felt terrible. His whole life seemed to him empty and futile. He sat all alone in his large, modern drawingroom which had been done up by an interior decorator and contained several modern paintings which Suraj secretly disliked; indeed, the whole room was only pleasant to him when it was full of his friends or had a big party going. He drank one whisky after the other. He perspired, he wept a little, his mind became soaked and soft. He heard the doorbell ring but he didn't take any notice and it rang again and he still didn't take any notice. Then Gwen and Maggie came in and said they'd been trying to phone and phone, and where had he been all the time and what was the matter? All his misery disappeared like a flash and he tried to rise to his feet but he was very unsteady and they said he had better sit down again. They sat down with him, one on each side. He tried to tell them a lot of things but his tongue was too big and furry. Finally he only waved his hand at them to express everything he wanted to but couldn't say and he cried a bit more but now it was with contentment. They suggested he should go to bed and he let them help him into his pyjamas, and when they had settled him and made him comfortable, he fell asleep at once with a smile of satisfaction on his face.

This incident drew them, if anything, closer together.

The girls did not speak about it much but neither did they try to avoid the subject, and whenever they referred to it, it was in a light, amused way. Suraj even became quite proud of it and felt it was a manly thing to get drunk and have to be put to bed. And now that they had seen him in this state, he felt there was nothing he need hide from them; he trusted them completely and wanted them to know everything about him, not only the things of which he was very proud but others also. He told them more and more about his early days, his childhood in a town in the North, his family who expected him to go to college and from whom in the end he had had to run away because they could never sympathise with his higher ambitions. He also told them a lot about his early days of hardship in Bombay, before he met his patron and began to do well : how he had attached himself to groups of people on the outskirts of the film industry and had followed them around and sat with them in cheap restaurants, hoping that someone would buy him a meal and yet so shy to accept it that often he had walked away the moment the menu was brought. He had lived with anyone who was ready to put him up, and there were always people who didn't mind if he unrolled his bedding on their veranda or, during the monsoon, in whatever space he could find inside; on hot nights he often slept out on the beach. His greatest fear was always that his family would find him before he had achieved what he wanted and had become rich and famous (he never had any doubts that he would). He missed them and wanted to be with them, but he dared not even write to them. Sometimes he did write to them but he never sent the letters, he crumpled them up and threw them away. He also wrote some poetry. He was often alone at that time and went for long walks and had many strange thoughts and feelings. Sometimes these thoughts were very happy and then he wouldn't walk but run on the empty beach and even cry out and jump into the air; but sometimes they were sad, and then he would lie down on the sand and bury his head in his arms and fall asleep like one falling into a heavy, unpleasant stupor. He spent his eighteenth birthday like that, alone and asleep.

Gwen and Maggie were eager to tell him about their lives too. Only they did not have very much to tell. Their present world tour was their first big adventure; before that they had simply been at boarding school and the holidays they had spent at home with their families or gone to stay on the Continent with family friends. They looked forward, however, to a lot of things happening to them in the future.

"What things?" Suraj asked them.

They smiled and looked thoughtful. They were on a deserted beach several miles out of town. Suraj had brought them here in his car, and he had also carried lunch along in a big picnic basket. There were chickens and fried pancakes stuffed with potatoes, and he had gone to a lot of trouble and managed to procure a bottle of champagne which he twirled lovingly in its ice bucket. He had wanted to bring a servant along to serve the food and make everything comfortable for them, but they said they preferred to manage on their own. Indeed, it was surprising how well they did manage. Whereas Suraj was inclined rather roughly to pull things out of the basket, throw away the paper and begin to eat, they first spread a scarf (he had forgotten, or rather, never thought of a tablecloth) and set everything out very nicely, and Gwen even took a few steps away to see what it looked like and then came back and touched up the arrangement with her long, pale hands.

They told him about what they hoped to do in London. They were both trying to persuade their families to let them take a flat together instead of living at home. They even described how they would furnish the flat with a Victorian chest-of-drawers and commercial posters on the walls. Gwen would keep a Siamese cat and Maggie a bull-terrier. They would probably go out a lot — they both liked dancing and good food in good restaurants — but they also expected to be at home quite often for Maggie wanted to learn Spanish and Gwen to do a lot of reading. They loved cooking and looked forward to making all sorts of delicious, unusual little dishes and entertaining their friends.

"What friends?" Suraj said with a knowing smile.

They shrugged and smiled back : "Just friends."

"Boy friends?"

"Those too, I expect," Maggie said with cheerful pleasure.

"Ah-ha!" said Suraj and winked; and when they didn't take him up on it, he said "I think in England all the girls have a lot of boy friends and they have a very good time together. Isn't it? Tell me. The truth now." He became quite roguish and even shook a finger at them, so that they both burst out laughing and said "Get along with you", in nasal cockney accents.

"Please don't try to put me off the scent," he said. "I know all about it. The parties where you switch the lights off and petting in cars and all that pre-marital sex. I think it's a very good thing. I believe in a free society, and I think it is a sign of backwardness when society is not free in this respect."

Maggie rolled around in the sand, from her stomach to her back, covering herself with tiny golden grains in the process. She said "Gwen didn't sleep with anyone till last year, but I was only fifteen. I developed early."

The expression on Suraj's face changed suddenly, utterly. Perhaps Maggie noticed, perhaps she didn't, but in any case she went on : "My first time wasn't terribly successful. It was at the end of the hols and I was feeling awful and wondering would school never stop, would nothing ever happen, and then I met this man in Kensington Gardens. You know how at that age one is absolutely panting for new experiences. But it didn't come up to expectations really. In fact, it was such a disappointment that it put me off sex for more than a year."

"Who is coming for a swim!" Suraj shouted with unnatural brightness and jumped up and dashed towards the sea. He was glad when they did not follow. He swam strongly, taking pleasure in battling against the waves. When he was tired, he lay on his back and floated, letting himself be carried out a little further than was quite wise. His mind and feelings were in turmoil. He found he could not bear the idea of the two girls with other men. Not because he was personally jealous but because it was outrageous to think of them that way : Maggie so wholesome, untouched,

E

firm-fleshed, and Gwen who was frail and pale and grown too tall like a girl who's been ill and lying in bed for a long time. They were not women, they were friends, his friends. He felt it was his duty to protect them, and it made him furious to think of them going back to England where he would no longer be able to do so and they would be prey to anyone who came along, to all those people who believed in pre-marital sex and other loose practices.

One day he decided to take them to his mother's house. They were surprised — they hadn't realised his mother was in Bombay, they thought she was still far away in the place from which he had run away. Now they learned that, after his father's death a few years ago, he had brought her and the rest of the family to Bombay and had bought a house for them and kept them there. He seemed shy to speak of all this and was indeed quite irritable, as if he resented having broken his silence on the subject. The two girls dressed up carefully in silk frocks and stockings and high-heeled shoes, so that they looked as if they were going to church. Suraj was rather silent and even a little surly all the way he drove them there, and his mood did not improve when they reached their destination. The house was large and full of women. There was not only his mother but also various unmarried sisters and a lot of old aunts and other dependents. They crowded round and touched and patted Suraj and said he was looking weak. A lot of food was brought, and the girls were urged to eat which they did — even the strangest and most out-rageous pickles — with their usual grateful enthusiasm. Everyone looked at them from top to toe and smiled

at them to show goodwill, and the girls smiled back;
only Suraj was frowning.

"Are you married?" one of the sisters asked the
girls in English. "Any children?"

"I'm afraid not," Gwen said. She stretched her hand
out for another fritter and murmured "Delicious," as
she popped it, piping hot, into her mouth.

"Look at that one," said an aunt in Hindi. "Thin
as a fish-bone, but how she eats."

They all laughed, and the girls too laughed though
they hadn't understood what was said. Suraj suddenly
shouted "Be quiet!" and hit his fist on the table. The
girls looked at him in surprise, but the relatives composed their faces and were quiet at once.

"Rest, son," said his mother. "Don't upset yourself." She stroked his hair and his cheeks soothingly;
an aunt kneeled on the floor and began to press his
ankles but he drew them away ungraciously. "Listen,"
said his mother; she put her hand secretively to the
side of her mouth and began to whisper in his ear.
He did not seem to like what he heard. Other
relatives came and whispered in his other ear. Suddenly
he stood up; he told the girls "Come on, we are going."

They held a glass of sherbet in one hand, a coloured
sweetmeat in the other. "What, already?"

"Come on."

He did not look like a person with whom one could
argue. They took a last gulp of their sherbet and
hastily ate up the remains of their sweetmeats. They
got up, still chewing, and dusting crumbs from their
hands.

"But you have eaten nothing!" cried the relatives.
They snatched up the platters of food and followed

the departing guests with them. "One little piece of
barfi," they pleaded. "Only to taste." Gwen and
Maggie lingered and looked willing enough, but Suraj
hustled them out of the house and into the car and
slammed the car-door after them decisively. He did
not speak to them much on the way home and left
them at their hotel with a curt, half-angry goodbye.

Next day he said to them aggressively "You don't
know anything about our Indian way of life."

"You didn't give us much time to find out," Gwen
said.

They were in the girls' hotel room, and Gwen was
lying on the bed with a book and Maggie sat in an
armchair with one foot drawn up and painting her
toenails silver.

"I could see you were very bored there," he said
after a while.

"Bored!"

"Yes." Then he said again : "You don't know anything about the way we live."

"We were having a simply marvellous time. Everyone
was so kind, and those fabulous sweets! Only you
were cross and disagreeable."

Suddenly he roared : "Because I was bored! Yes,
it was I! I was bored! Very bored!" He turned from
the window and glared at his two friends as if he
hated them. Embarrassed by so much strong feeling,
Maggie blushed and bent her head closer over her
toenails. Gwen too avoided looking at Suraj.

"Our Indian families are like that," he said. "What
do you know of it. Yes, I love them but — they want
so much! They eat me up! You know nothing."

He wandered to their dressingtable and absentmindedly sprayed himself from one of the bottles. A dewy English flower-smell enveloped him and he liked it and sprayed himself some more. This seemed to calm him.

"How did you like the house?" he said. "I bought it for them for six lakhs of rupees. And the furniture? Do you think it is in good taste?"

"It looked awfully comfortable."

"They want a silver tea-set." He laughed. "And another car. They say they need two. Supposing someone wants to go shopping and another person wants to go to the temple, then what? They quarrel a lot about the car. Do your families also have many quarrels?"

The two girls looked at each other and began to laugh. Gwen said "They have differences of opinion. It's very subtle."

"First thing when I go there I have to hear about all the quarrels. Next thing I have to hear is the girls they have found for me to marry. Ooph! It's always the same : after half an hour I want to run away and then they begin to cry and then I stay. What sort of people we are! I think you must be having a good laugh at us."

He sprayed himself again from the atomiser, he worked the lever up and down vigorously so that a lot of scent came out and enveloped him in a cool, fragrant mist. Maggie, whose bottle it was, cried "Hey!"

"I like it." He took out some more and shut his eyes with pleasure. "Yesterday they again had a girl for me. Very good family, very pretty, sixteen years old. I wanted to say : But I'm going to marry these two! Only to see the fun. And why not?" he said suddenly. "Why shouldn't I marry you two? I can do what I like. We can all stay together in my apartment, there are many rooms I never use. Or I will build a new house for us — yes, I'll do that, a brandnew house to most modern design!" He became enthusiastic. He imagined himself always enveloped in an atmosphere of English floral scent. He would buy English clothes for them. They would have a cook who knew how to prepare all English dishes. "Will you like it?" he asked them. "Do you think it will be nice." But although they said it would be wonderful, he frowned and said "No, you wouldn't like it. You don't want to stay here. You think our poor India is very backward."

He was often dissatisfied nowadays. He had always enjoyed being surrounded by his friends and talking and laughing with them and having them run little errands for him. Now he tired of them quickly, and in the middle of a friendly session — drinking, joking, having fun — he would tell them to go away. They were surprised, and he was surprised himself; and when they had gone, he wandered round the big, empty apartment by himself and wished for them back again. He had become used to having many people laugh when he made a joke and hearing from them what a big actor he was and how much better than all his rivals. He wanted to hear that, he needed it. Yet, all the same, when they said it now, he became irritated with them. Their jokes too no longer amused him, and the whole tenor of their conversation — which he had lived on and thrived on, which had been *his* — now often filled him with boredom and even disgust. It was the same not only with his friends but with his mistresses too. Everything that had once excited him about them now had the opposite effect. Their intensely feminine being — their soft, fat bodies, their long oiled hair, the heavy, heady Indian perfumes they used, the transparent sari drawn coyly over the enticing cleft that emerged from their low-cut blouses, the little jingle that rang out from bracelets and anklets and golden chains as they moved, their demure, clinging, giggling ways, their little sulks and tantrums — all this, which had once spelled everything feminine and desirable to him, now affected him unpleasantly. As a result, he was tough with his girls, sometimes brutal, and deliberately picked quarrels with them.

But he also quarrelled with Gwen and Maggie. He felt obscurely that they were the cause of his dissatisfaction with what had up till now been a satisfying or, at any rate, an enviable life. Although they never uttered a critical word, he thought of them as critical, as setting themselves up as superior, and it angered him. He defended things against them that they had never attacked and had no thoughts of attacking. These ranged from his family to the Bombay film industry to the whole of India which he admitted was not very advanced in the material sense but which amply made up for this shortcoming by the richness of its spiritual heritage. The two girls did not deny it, in fact they even agreed with him — politely rather than enthusiastically : they had not come here on any higher quest but were ready to concede that such a quest was possible, indeed they knew that many people came on it. Yet their agreement far from soothing only exasperated him further for it made him feel as if they were humouring him. Then he would turn right round and say that no, India *was* poor and backward, he felt ashamed when he thought of how far behind it lagged other countries like England and America and also when he thought of the starving people in the streets and the fact that after so many years of Independence no further progress had been made : but of course, he said, they wouldn't understand that, they were only foreigners and could have no conception of the deep feelings that an Indian had for his country. The girls took these changes of mood very well although sometimes, if he carried on for too long a time or at too high a pitch, they said "Oh do shut up, Suraj," but so calmly, even patiently, that there was no offence in it. Indeed, when they said that, he at once stopped talking that way and became instead extremely attentive and proposed all sorts of outings and other amusements for them and did everything he could to make amends and show them how much he cared for them. But one thing he could not bear and that was when they talked of going away. He had already made them cancel a visit to Isphahan they had planned on their way back, and now he kept persuading them to postpone going home to England, even though their parents and their jobs were waiting for them there and anxious letters were already beginning to arrive.

He wanted them with him everywhere nowadays. Even when they would have much preferred to stay doing nothing on the beach, he made them come and watch him shooting or took them along to some film-world function that he had to attend. But he did not like to see them enjoying themselves too much there. If he noticed them talking too long to any one person, he would come and take them away to meet someone else; and afterwards he would ask them, "What were you talking so much to him?" and while they were trying to recollect what had been said (which was rarely interesting enough to remember), he went on to suggest, "It is best not to know such people very well."

"But, Suraj, he was charming!"

"Yes, yes, for you he must have put on a very nice face."

"Oh dear. What's he done then? What's the matter with him?"

But Suraj would not tell them. He became indeed rather prim and said it was not necessary for them to know such things, and all their entreaties could not unseal his lips any further. Then they became exasperated, furious with him, but he enjoyed that and laughed with pleasure at the names they called him.

A producer gave a party in the banquet-room of a big hotel. Everyone was there. Long buffet tables had been laid out with huge platters of pilao, lobster and prawn curries, mountains of kebabs heaped with sliced raw onions. The less important guests jostled and pushed each other in piling up their plates as if they had never eaten before and would perhaps never eat again. Streamers and paper lanterns festooned the ceiling, and everything was done just as it should be for the management of the hotel had plenty of practice in putting on these kind of parties. In deference to the prohibition laws, drinks were served — with a secrecy which had become ostentatious and pleasurable — in a little side-room to which many people took many trips and always came back with a wink and a joke

("They are serving very good coca-colas in there").
The producer was in an excellent mood to see his
party going so well. He rallied everyone to momentous
feats of eating and drinking, joked and slapped backs,
clapped his hands with enjoyment, was simultaneously
paternal and slyly jovial with all the actresses in white
saris. He made a big fuss of Gwen and Maggie who
were not really enjoying themselves much — they had
been to too many parties like this one by now — but
pretended they were. Later there was music, and a
playback singer rendered a love-song with so much
feeling that it made people shake their heads at the
beauty of life and filled them with sadness and
longing. The host turned to Gwen and Maggie and
asked "Did you like it?" They saw that his eyes were
swimming in tears.

"Jolly nice," they replied, embarrassed for him and
tactfully looking the other way.

He was not ashamed but proud of his tears : "What
songs we have," he said, "what feeling," and since
further words failed him, he shut his eyes and pressed
his heart where it hurt· him. But then he became
cheerful again and, putting an arm round the waist
of each girl, said: "Now we would like to hear an
English song."

Gwen and Maggie looked at each other over the
top of his head. They gave the tiniest shrug, their
eyebrows were ever so slightly raised.

People clapped and shouted "Yes yes! Let us have
a Beatle song!"

But what Gwen and Maggie chose to give was
not a Beatle song. An imperceptible sign passed
between them, and then they stood side by side

very correctly, and began to sing :
> Go, stranger! track the deep,
> Free, free, the white sails spread!
> Wave may not foam, nor wild wind sweep,
> Where rest not England's dead.

They sang the way they had been taught at school, with spirit and expression. They lifted their heads and their voices high and every time the refrain came round they made a conductor's gesture with their hands as if encouraging their audience to join in. Each rhythmically tapped a foot on the floor. It was rousing and stirring and brave. When they had finished, there was tremendous applause. Many people were laughing; some of the actresses had taken out little lace handkerchiefs and tittered into them. The producer was enchanted, he stretched up and kissed their cheeks and he squeezed their hips ("But how *thin* you are," he whispered, deeply concerned, when he had done this to Gwen). The girls accepted the applause with a graceful mixture of pride and modesty. They knew their performance could not be judged by the highest standards, but they were happy to have given pleasure. They avoided looking at Suraj.

All the way home in his car he upbraided, scolded them. "Why did you do it?" he said several times. "Because we were asked," they replied, but when he kept repeating his question, they were silent and looked out of the car window at the lights stretching like jewels all round the sea-front.

"Everyone was laughing at you," he said.

"So what."

He groaned; he seemed in real pain. "And not only laughing . . . Gwen, Maggie, you don't know what these people are. What thoughts they have." When they didn't answer but went on looking out of the window, he said desperately "Especially about English girls."

"I nearly got stuck in that Egypt's burning plain bit," Maggie said to Gwen.

"I know you did."

"But it went rather well on the whole, don't you think?"

"Frightfully well. I'm proud of us."

"They think all English girls are loose in their morals," Suraj said. "When they look at you, they laugh because of the thoughts they have about you. Such dirty thoughts."

"Oh do shut up, Suraj."

"Yes, when truth is to be heard then you say shut up."

But he did not speak again. He sat between the two of them with his arms folded and staring grimly ahead of him at the back of his chauffeur's neck. He did not move even when they reached the hotel and the girls got out, nor did he answer to their cheerful good-nights. He was angry with them.

But next day he turned up in great excitement at the hotel. A famous American saxophone-player was passing through Bombay, and Suraj had got three tickets. "You try and get tickets on your own," he said triumphantly. "Only try. Even if you pay Rs.500 on the black market you won't be able to get."

"You are clever." Then they asked : "When is it?"

"On the fifteenth."

They smiled sadly and told him that they had booked their return tickets for the twelfth. Suraj was thunderstruck. He looked from one to the other. He said "It is because I was angry with you in the car."

"Of course not," they said, laughing a little uneasily and avoiding his eyes.

He insisted it was. He accused himself for his bad temper and then accused them for taking such spiteful revenge on him. He wouldn't listen when they tried to tell him that it was time they went home, they couldn't stay here for ever, and that their decision had nothing to do with what had happened the night before. He knew that wasn't true and wanted to draw them out to admit it. But they just kept on saying no, they had to go, and no, it wasn't because of anything he had said or done. Then he tried to persuade them at least to postpone their departure by two weeks, one week — all right, not a week, just a few days, just till the concert — but here too they would not budge from their position.

Finally he changed. He became resigned and deeply melancholy and recognised that the pain of parting had to be endured. This attitude remained with him in the days that were left. He sighed often, and quoted Urdu couplets about the tears of friends whose paths lie in separate directions. This led him further, and he became even more philosophical and quoted verses about the transience of all worldly pleasures and how nothing ever stayed — not the song of the nightingale nor the bloom of the rose nor the throne of kings — but everything dissolved and disappeared as if it had never been. The girls too became depressed, they said "It's going to be awful without you." When they said that, he became more cheerful and made plans for the future : how they would come back again, or he would go and visit them in England, and meanwhile, of course, there would be letters, many many letters, between them.

The girls did write very often. He loved getting their letters which were very lively and were just the way they spoke. He marvelled at the way they could write like that. When he himself sat down to write, the words came out stiff like words that are written not like words that are spoken. And when he had put down that he was well and hoped that they were also and that the weather was not good and that he was going up to Simla to shoot some scenes in snow, then he didn't know what else to say. Their letters were filled with so many things that happened to them — how they had discovered a marvellous little new restaurant, and that skirts were so short now that they had had to take up all their hems — but he could not think of anything to write. Nothing new ever happened to him : it was just shooting, and sitting with his friends, and premieres, always the same. It was not worth writing in a letter all the way to England. He would start writing — slowly and laboriously, with his lips moving — and then he would stop and not know what to say next. When he came back to it a few days later and read it over again, he was dissatisfied because it did not sound very well, nor was he sure of his spelling, and then he tore the letter up and told himself he would start again to-morrow. In the end he didn't write at all, and after a time their letters stopped too.

Sometimes his friends talked about the two English girls. At first they did so hesitantly, looking at him out of the corner of their eyes, but when he said nothing they became bolder and soon they were laughing and everyone had something humorous to contribute. Suraj smiled goodnaturedly and allowed himself to be teased. He did not contradict when they made references to events that had never happened, or assumed that there had been more than there actually had been. Sometimes he wondered to himself that there had not been more. At the time he had been proud of this fact, of the purity of their friendship; now he felt slightly ashamed of it, and would not have liked his friends to know. It was like a shortcoming, or like having been cheated. He did not understand how he could have allowed it to happen, and a hint of resentment entered into his memory of the English girls. Indeed, he did not like to think of them much any more, and whenever he could not help doing so, he would go out and visit one of his actress friends.

*   *   *

Rose Petals

He loves being a cabinet minister, he thinks it's wonderful. His bearer comes to wake him with tea early in the morning, and he gets up and starts getting dressed, ready to see the stream of callers who have already begun to gather downstairs. He thinks I'm still asleep but I'm awake and know what he is doing. Sometimes I peep at him as he moves around our bedroom. How fat and old he has become; and he makes an important face even when he is alone like this and thinks no one is watching him. He frowns and thinks of all his great affairs. Perhaps he is rehearsing a speech in Parliament. I see his lips move and sometimes he shakes his head and makes a gesture as if he were talking to someone. He struggles into his cotton tights; he still has not quite got used to these Indian clothes but he wears nothing else now. There was a time when only suits made in London were good enough for him. Now they hang in the closet, and no one ever wears them.

I don't get up till several hours later, when he has left the house. I don't like to get up early, and anyway there is nothing to do. I lie in bed with the curtains drawn. They are golden-yellow in colour, like honey, and so is the carpet, and the cushions and everything; because of this the light in the room is also honey-coloured. After a while Mina comes in. She sits on the bed and talks to me. She is fully dressed and very clean and tidy. She usually has breakfast with her father; she pours the tea for him and any guests there might be and takes an interest in what is being said. She too likes it that her father is a cabinet minister. She wants to be helpful to him in his work and reads all the newspapers and is very well up in current affairs. She intends to go back to college and take a course in political science and economics. We discuss this while she is sitting on my bed. She holds my hand in hers and plays with it. Her hand is broader than mine, and she cuts her nails short and does not use any varnish or anything. I look up into her face. It is so young and earnest; she frowns a little bit the way her father does when he is talking of something serious. I love her so much that I have to shut my eyes. I say "Kiss me, darling." She bends down to do so. She smells of Palmolive soap.

By the time I get up, Mina too has left the house. She has many interests and activities. I'm alone in the house now with the servants. I get up from my bed and walk over to the dressing-table to see myself in the mirror there. I always do this first thing when I get up. It is a habit that has remained with me from the past when I was very interested in my appearance and took so much pleasure in looking in the mirror that I would jump eagerly out of bed to see myself. Now this pleasure has gone. If I don't look too closely and with the curtains drawn and the room all honey-coloured, I don't appear so very different from what I used to be. But sometimes I'm in a mischievous mood with myself. I stretch out my hand and lift the yellow silk curtain. The light comes streaming in straight on to the mirror, and now yes I can see that I do look very different from the way I used to.

Biju comes every day. Often he is already sitting

F

there when I come down. He is reading the papers, but only the cinema and restaurant advertisements and perhaps the local news if there has been a murder or some interesting social engagement. He usually stays all day. He has nowhere to go and nothing to do. Every day he asks "And how is the Minister?" Every day he makes fun of him. I enjoy that, and I also make fun of him with Biju. They are cousins but they have always been very different. Biju likes a nice life, no work, good food and drinking. The Minister also likes good food and drinking, but he can't sit like Biju in a house with a woman all day. He always has to be doing something or he becomes restless and his temper is spoiled. Biju's temper is never spoiled although sometimes he is melancholy; then he recites sad poetry or plays sad music on the gramophone.

Quite often we have a lunch or dinner party in the house. Of course it is always the Minister's party and the guests are all his. There are usually one or two cabinet ministers, an ambassador, a few newspaper editors — people like that. Biju likes to stay for these parties, I don't know why, they are not very interesting. He moves round the room talking to everyone. Biju looks distinguished — he is tall and well-built, and though the top of his head is mostly bald he keeps long side-burns; he is always well-dressed in an English suit, just like the Minister used to wear before taking to Indian clothes. The guests are impressed with Biju and talk to him as if he were as clever and important as they themselves are. They never guess that he is not because he speaks in a very grand English accent and is ready to talk on any subject they like.

Mina also enjoys her father's parties and she mingles

with the guests and listens to the intelligent conversation. But I don't enjoy them at all. I talk to the wives, but it is tiring for me to talk with strangers about things that are not interesting to me; very soon I slip away, hoping they will think that I have to supervise the servants in the kitchen. Actually, I don't enter the kitchen at all — there is no need because our cooks have been with us a long time; instead I lie down on a sofa somewhere or sit in the garden where no one can find me. Only Biju does find me sooner or later, and then he stays with me and talks to me about the guests. He imitates the accent of a foreign ambassador or shows how one of the cabinet ministers cracks nuts and spits out the shells. He makes me laugh, and I like being there with him in the garden which is so quiet with the birds all asleep in the trees and the moon shining down with a silver light. I wish we didn't have to go back. But I know that if I stay away too long, the Minister will miss me and get annoyed and send Mina to look for me. And when she has found us, she too will be annoyed — she will stand there and look at us severely as if we were two children that were not to be trusted.

Mina is often annoyed with us. She lectures us. Sometimes she comes home earlier than usual and finds me lying on a sofa and Biju by my side with a drink in one hand and a cigar in the other. She says "Is this all you ever do?"

Biju says "What else *is* there to do?"

"Aren't you awful." But she can't concentrate on us just now. She is very hungry and is wondering what to eat. I ring for the bearer and order refreshments to be brought for Mina on a tray. She sits with us while she is eating. After a while she feels fit enough to speak

to us again. She asks "Don't you want to do something constructive?"

Biju thinks about this for a while. He examines the
tip of his cigar while he is thinking; then he says "No."

"Well you ought to. Everybody ought to. There's
such a lot to do! In every conceivable field." She licks
crumbs off the ends of her fingers — I murmur automa-
tically "Darling, use the napkin" — and when she has
got them clean she uses them to tick off with : "Social.
Educational. Cultural — that reminds me : are you
coming to the play?"

"What play?"

"I've been telling you for *weeks*."

"Oh yes of course," I say. "I remember." I don't
really, but I know vaguely that her friends are always
putting on advanced plays translated from French or
German or Roumanian. Mina has no acting talent herself but she takes great interest in these activities. She
often attends rehearsals, and as the time of the performance draws near, she is busy selling tickets and
persuading shopkeepers to allow her to stick posters
in their windows.

"This is really going to be something special. It's a
difficult play but terribly interesting, and Bobo Oberoi
is just great as God the Father. What talent he has,
that boy, oh." She sighs with admiration, but next
moment she has recollected something and is looking
suspiciously at Biju and me : "You're welcome to buy
tickets of course, and I'm certainly going to sell you
some, but I hope you'll behave better than last time."

Biju looks guilty. It's true he didn't behave very well
last time. It was a long play, and again a difficult one.
Biju got restless — he sighed and crossed his long legs

now one way and now another and kept asking me how
much longer it was going to be. At last he decided to
go out and smoke and pushed his way down the row
so that everybody had either to get up or to squeeze
in their legs to let him pass, while he said "Excuse me"
in a loud voice and people in the rows behind said "Sh."

"Why don't they put on one of these nice musical
plays?" Biju asks now, as Mina eats the last biscuit
from her tray and washes it down with her glass of
milk. She doesn't answer him, but looks exasperated.
"My Fair Lady," Biju presses on. *"Funny Girl."* The
expression on Mina's face becomes more exasperated,
and I tell him to be quiet.

"If you'd only make an *effort,*" Mina says, doing
her best to be patient and in a voice that is almost
pleading. "To move with the times. To understand the
modern mind."

I try to excuse us : "We're too old, darling."

"It's nothing to do with age. It's an attitude, that's
all. Now look at Daddy."

"Ah," says Biju.

"He's the same age as you are."

"Two years older," Biju says.

"So you see."

Biju raises his glass as if he were drinking to someone, and as he does so, his face becomes so solemn and
respectful that it is difficult for me not to laugh.

The Minister is very keen to "move with the times."
It has always been one of his favourite sayings. Even
when he was young and long before he entered politics,
he was never satisfied doing what everyone else did —
looking after the estates, hunting and other sports,

entertaining guests — no, it was not enough for him.
When we were first married, he used to give me long lectures like Mina does now — about the changing times
and building up India and everyone putting their shoulder to the wheel — he would talk to me for a long time
on this subject, getting all the time more and more
excited and enthusiastic; only I did not listen too
carefully because, as with Mina, I was so happy only
looking at him while he talked that it didn't matter
to me what he said. How handsome he was in those
days! His eyes sparkled, and he was tall and strong
and always appeared to be in a great hurry as if difficult tasks awaited him. When he went up any stairs
it was two, three steps at a time, doors banged behind
him, his voice was loud and urgent like a king in battle
even when he was only calling to the servant for his
shoes. He used to get very impatient with me because
he said I was slow and lazy like an elephant, and if he
was walking behind me, he would prod my hips (which
were always rather heavy) and say "Get moving." In
those days he wanted me to do everything with him.
At one time he had imported a new fertiliser which
was going to do magic, and together we would walk
through the fields to see its effect (which was not
good : it partially killed the maize crop). Another
time we travelled to Japan to study their system of
hotel management because he thought of converting
one of our houses into a hotel. Then he had an idea
that he would like to start a factory for manufactu-
ring steel tubing, and we went to Russia to observe the
process of manufacture. Wherever we went, he drew
up a heavy programme for us which I found very
tiring; but since he himself never needed any rest, he

couldn't understand why I should. He began to feel that I was a hindrance to him on these tours, and as the years went by, he became less eager to take me with him.

Fortunately, just at that time Biju came back from abroad and he began to spend a lot of time with me so I did not feel too lonely. It was said in the family that Biju had been abroad all these years to study, but of course it was well known that he had not done much studying. Even at that age he was very lazy and did not like to do anything except enjoy himself and have a good time. In the beginning, when he first came back, he used to go to Bombay quite often, to meet with friends and dance and go to the races, but later he did not care so much for these amusements and came to stay on his land which was near to ours, or — during the summer when we went up to Simla — he also took a house there. Everyone was keen for him to get married, and his aunts were always finding suitable girls for him. But he didn't like any of them. He says it is because of me that he didn't marry, but that's only his excuse. It is just that he was too lazy to take up any burdens.

It is not easy to be a Minister's wife. People ask me to do all sorts of things that I don't like to do. They ask me to sit on welfare committees and give away prizes at cultural shows. I want to say no, but the Minister says it's my duty, so I go. But I do it very badly. All the other ladies are used to sitting on committees and they make speeches and know exactly what is wanted. Sometimes they get very heated, especially when they have to elect one another on to

sub-committees. They all want to be on as many
committees and sub-committees as possible. Not for
any selfish reasons but because they feel it is necessary
for the good of India. Each proves to the other point
by point how necessary it is and they hotly debate
with one another. Sometimes they turn to me to ask
my opinion, but I don't have any opinion, I don't
know what it is they are discussing. Then they turn
away from me again and go on talking to each other,
and although they are polite to me, I know they don't
have a high opinion of me and think I'm not worthy
to be a Minister's wife. I wish Mina could be there
instead of me. She would be able to talk like they do,
and they would respect her.

When I have to give a speech anywhere, it is always
Mina who writes it for me. She writes a beautiful
speech and then she makes me rehearse it. She is
very thorough and strict with me. "No!" she cries,
"Not 'today each of us carries a burden of responsibility', but 'each of us carries a burden of *responsibility*'!" I start again and say it the way she wants
me to say it, and as many times as she wants me to till
at last she is satisfied. She is never entirely satisfied :
at the end of each rehearsal, she sighs and looks at me
with doubtful eyes. And she is right to be doubtful
because, when the time comes to make the speech, I
forget all about our rehearsal and just read it off as
quickly as possible. When I come home, she asks me
how did it go, and I tell her that everyone praised the
speech and said it was full of beautiful words and
thoughts.

But once she was with me. It was a school's sports
day, and it was really quite nice, not like some of the

other functions I have had to attend. We all sat on chairs in the school grounds and enjoyed the winter sunshine. Mina and I sat in the front row with the headmistress and the school governors and some other people who had been introduced to us but I could not remember who they were. The girls did mass PT, and rhythmic exercises, and they ran various races. They were accompanied by the school band, and one of the teachers announced each item over the microphone which, however, was not in good order so that the announcement could not be heard very well. From time to time the headmistress explained something to me, and I nodded and smiled although — because of the noise from the loudspeaker and the band — I could not hear what she said. The sun was warm on my face, and I half shut my eyes, and the girls were a pretty coloured blur. Mina nudged me and whispered "Mummy, are you falling asleep?" so I opened my eyes again quickly and clapped loudly at the conclusion of an item and turned to smile at the headmistress who smiled back to me.

When it was time for my speech, I got up quite happily and read it from the paper Mina had got ready for me. The microphone crackled very loudly so I don't think my speech could be heard distinctly, but no one seemed to mind. I didn't mind either. Then I gave away the prizes, and it was all over and we could go home. I was cheerful and relieved, as I always am when one of these functions is finished, but as soon as we were alone in the car together, Mina began to reproach me for the way I had delivered the speech. She was upset not because I had spoiled her speech — that didn't matter, she said — but because I hadn't cared about it; I hadn't cared about the whole function; I was not serious. "You even fell asleep," she accused me.

"No no, the sun was in my eyes, so I shut them."

"Why are you like that? You and Uncle Biju. Nothing is serious for you. Life is just a game."

I was silent. I was sorry that she was so disappointed in me. We rode along in silence. My head was turned away from her. I looked out of the window but saw nothing. From time to time a sigh escaped my lips. Then, after a while, she laid her hand on mine. I pressed it, and she came closer and put her head on my shoulder. How sweetly she forgave me, how affectionately she clung to me. I laid my lips against her hair and kissed it again and again.

Is life only a game for Biju and me? I don't know. It's true, we laugh a lot together and have jokes which Mina says are childish. The Minister also gets impatient with us, although we are always careful not to laugh too much when he is there. He himself is of course very serious. The important face with which I see him get up in the morning remains with him till he goes to bed at night. But, in spite of all the great affairs with which his day is filled, once he is in bed he falls asleep at once and his face next to me on the pillow is peaceful like a child's. I toss and turn for many hours, and although I try not to, I usually have to take one of my pills. Biju also has to sleep with pills. And he has terrible nightmares. Often his servant has to rush into his bedroom because he hears him screaming with fear and he shakes him by the shoulder and shouts "Sahib, Sahib!" till Biju wakes up. Terrible things happen in Biju's dreams : he falls down mountain-sides, tigers jump through his window, he is publicly hanged on a gallows. When his servant shakes him awake, he is trembling all over and wet with perspiration. But he is glad to be awake and alive.

Nothing like that ever happens in the Minister's dreams. He has no dreams. When he goes to sleep at night, there is a complete blank till he wakes up again in the morning and starts to do important things. He always says that he has a great number of worries — his whole life he tells me is one big worry, and some-times he feels as if he has to carry all the problems of the government and the country on his own shoulders — but all the same he sleeps so soundly. He never seems to be troubled by the sort of thoughts that come to me. Probably he doesn't have time for them. I see him look into the mirror but he appears to do so with pleasure, pulling down his coat and smoothing his hair and turning this way and that to see himself sideways. He smiles at what he sees, he-likes it. I wonder — doesn't he remember what he was? How can he like that fat old man that now looks back at him?

It is strange that when you're young you don't think that it can ever happen to you that you'll get old. Or perhaps you do think about it but you don't really believe it, not in your heart of hearts. I remem-ber once we were talking about it, many years ago, Biju and I. We were staying in a house we have by a lake. We never used this house much because it was built as a shooting-box and none of us cared for hunt-ing and shooting. In fact, the Minister had definitely renounced them on what he called humanitarian grounds, and he was always telling people about these grounds and had even printed a pamphlet about them; only it had been done very badly by the local printers and had so many spelling mistakes in it that the Minister felt ashamed and didn't want it distributed. That time we were staying in the shooting-box because he had come on an inspection tour. These inspection tours were another favourite idea of his. He always came on them without any advance notice so as to keep the people who looked after the properties alert all the year round. Sometimes he took a whole party of guests with him, but that time it was only he and I and Biju who had come with us because he thought he would be bored alone at home.

The Minister — of course he wasn't a Minister at that time — was busy going over the house, running his finger along ledges for dust and inspecting dinner services that hadn't been in use for twenty years, while Biju and I rested after our journey in the small red sittingroom. This room had many ornaments in it that my father-in-law, who frequently travelled to Europe, had brought back with him. There were views of Venice in golden frames on the walls, and an ormolu clock on the mantelpiece, and next to it a lacquered musical box that intrigued Biju very much. He kept playing it over and over again. The house was built on a lake and the light from the water filled the room and was reflected from the glass of the pictures of Venice so that the walls appeared to be swaying and rippling as if waves were passing over them. The music box played a very sweet sad tinkling little tune, and Biju didn't seem to get tired of it and I didn't either; indeed, the fact that it was being played over and over again somehow made it even sweeter and sadder so that all sorts of thoughts and feelings rose in the heart. We were drinking orange squash.

Biju said "How do you think it'll be when we're old?"

This question was perhaps sudden but I understood how it had come into his head at that particular moment. I said "Same as now."

"We'll always be sitting like this?"

"Why not."

At that time it wasn't possible for me to think of Biju as old. He was very slim and had a mop of hair and wore a trim little moustache. He was a wonderful dancer and knew all the latest steps. When he heard a snatch of dance music on the radio, at once his feet tapped up and down.

He wound the music box again, and the sad little tune played. The thought of being together like this for ever — always in some beautiful room with a view from its long windows of water or a lawn; or hot summer nights in a garden full of scents and overlaid with moonlight so white that it looked like snow — the thought of it was sad and yet also quite nice. I couldn't really think of us as old : only the same as we were now with, at the most, white hair.

"What about the Revolution?" I asked.

Biju laughed : "No, then we won't be here at all." He put his head sideways and showed a rope going round his neck : "Up on a lamp-post."

The Revolution was one of our jokes. I don't know whether we really thought it would come. I think often we felt it ought to come, but when we talked about it, it was only to laugh and joke. The Minister did sometimes talk about it seriously, but he didn't believe in it. He said India would always remain a parliamentary democracy because that was the best mode of government. Once all three of us were driving in a car when we were held up by some policemen. They were very polite and apologised and asked us please to take another road because some slum houses were being demolished on this one. Our chauffeur tried to reverse but the gear was stuck and for a while we couldn't move. Out of our car window we could see a squad of demolition workers knocking down the hovels made of old tins and sticks and rags, and the people who lived in the hovels picking up what they could from among the debris. They didn't look angry, just sad, except for one old woman who was shaking her fist and shouting something that we couldn't hear. She ran around and got in the way of the workers till someone gave her a push and she fell over. When she got up, she was holding her knee and limping but she had stopped shouting and she too began to dig among the debris. The Minister was getting very impatient with the car not starting, and he was busy giving instructions to the chauffeur. When at last we managed to get away, he talked all the time about the car and that it was a faulty model — all the models of that year were — cars were like vintages he said, some years were good, some not so good. I don't think Biju was paying any more attention than I was. He didn't say anything that time, but later in the day he was making a lot of jokes about the Revolution and how we would all be strung up on lamp-posts or perhaps, if we were lucky, sent to work in the salt-mines. The Minister said "What salt-mines? At least get your facts straight."

But to go back to that time in the shooting-box.

After finishing his inspection tour, the Minister came striding into the room and asked "What are you doing?" and when we told him we were talking about our old age, he said "Ah," as if he thought it might be a good subject for discussion. He liked people to have discussions and got impatient with Biju and me because we never had any.

"When I think of my old age," he said, "I think mainly : what will I have achieved? That means, what sort of person will I be? Because a person can only be judged by his achievements." He walked up and down the room, playing an imaginary game of tennis : he served imaginary balls hard across an imaginary net, stretching up so that his chest swelled out. "I hope I'll have done something," he said as he served. "I intend to. I intend to be a very busy person. Not only when I'm young but when I'm old too." He kept on serving and with such energy that he got a bit out of breath. "Right-till-the-end," he said, slamming a particularly hard ball.

"Out," Biju said.

The Minister turned on him with indignation. "Absolutely in," he said. "And turn off that damn noise, it's getting on my nerves." Biju shut the music box.

"I'll tell you something else," said the Minister. "The point about old age is not to be afraid of it. To meet it head-on. As a challenge that, like everything else, has to be faced and won. The King of Sweden played tennis at the age of *ninety*. I intend to be like that."

How pleased he would have been at that time if he

had known that he was going to be a cabinet minister. Things have not really turned out very different from the way we thought they would. The Minister is busy, and Biju and I are not. We sit in the room and look out into the garden, or sit in the garden and enjoy the trees and flowers. But being old does not mean only white hair. As a matter of fact, we neither of us have all that much white hair (Miss Yvonne takes care of mine, and Biju has lost most of his anyway). We still talk the way we used to, and laugh and joke, but — no, it is not true that life is a game for us. When we were young, we even enjoyed being sad — like when we listened to the music box — and now even when we're laughing, I don't know that we really *are* laughing. Only it is not possible for us to be serious the way the Minister is, and Mina.

Everyone nowadays is serious — all the people who come to the house, and the ladies on committees — they are for ever having discussions and talking about important problems. The Minister of course likes it very much, and he hardly ever stops talking. He gives long interviews to the Press and addresses meetings and talks on the radio, and he is always what he calls "threshing out his ideas" with the people who come to see him and those who come to our parties and with Mina and with Mina's friends. He especially enjoys talking to Mina's friends, and no wonder because they hang on every word he says, and although they argue quite a lot with him, they do so in a very respectful way. He gets carried away talking to them and forgets the time so that his secretary has to come and remind him; then he jumps up with a shout of surprise and humorously scolds them for keeping him from his duties; and they all laugh and say "Thank you, sir", and Mina kisses his cheek and is terribly proud of him.

The Minister says it is good to be with young people and listen to their ideas. He says it keeps the mind flexible and conditions it to deal with the problems of tomorrow as well as those of today. Biju too would like to talk to Mina's friends. I see him go into the room in which they are all sitting. Before he goes in, he pats his tie, and smoothes his hair to look extra smart. But as a matter of fact he looks rather too smart. He is wearing an English suit and has a handkerchief scented with eau-de-cologne arranged artistically in his top pocket. He seems taller than everyone else in the room. He begins to make conversation. He says "Any of you seen the new film at the Odeon?" in his clipped, very English accent that always impresses the people at the Minister's parties. But these young people are not impressed. They even look puzzled as if they have not understood what he said, and he repeats his question. They are polite young people and they answer him politely. But no one is at ease. Biju also is embarrassed; he clears his throat and flicks his hand-kerchief out of his pocket and holds it against his nose for a moment as if to sniff the eau-de-cologne. But he doesn't want to go away, he wants to go on talking. He begins to tell them some long story. Perhaps it is about the film, perhaps it is about a similar film he has once seen, perhaps it is some incident from his past life. It goes on for a long time. Sometimes Biju laughs in the middle and he is disappointed when no one laughs with him. He flicks out his handkerchief again and sniffs it. His story doesn't come to an end; it has no end, he simply trails off and says "Yes". The young

G

people patiently wait to see if he wants to say anything more. He looks as if he does want to say more,
but before he can do so, Mina says "Oh Uncle, I think
I hear Mummy calling you." Biju seems as relieved as
everyone else to have an excuse to go away.

Once Mina and her friends rolled up the carpet in
the drawingroom and danced to records. The doors of
the drawingroom were wide open and the light and
music came out into the garden where Biju and I were.
We sat on a stone bench by the fountain and looked
at them. They were stamping and shaking from side to
side in what I suppose were the latest dances. We
stayed and watched them for a long time. Biju was
very interested, he craned forward and sometimes he
said "Did you see that?" and sometimes he gave a
short laugh as if he didn't believe what he saw. I was
only interested in looking at Mina. She was stamping
and shaking like all the rest, and she had taken off
her shoes and flung her veil over her shoulders so that
it danced behind her. She laughed and turned and
sometimes flung up her arms into the air.

Biju said "Care to dance?" and when I shook my
head, he jumped up from the bench and began to
dance by himself. He tried to do it the way they were
doing inside. He couldn't get it right, but he kept on
trying. He wanted me to try too, but I wouldn't.
"Come on," he said, partly to me, partly to himself,
as he tried to get his feet and his hips to make the
right movements. He was getting out of breath but he
wouldn't give up. I was worried that he might strain
his heart, but I didn't say anything because he never
likes to be reminded of his heart. Suddenly he said
"There, now see!" and indeed when I looked he was

doing it absolutely right, just like they were doing inside. Only he looked more graceful than they did because probably he was a better dancer. He was enjoying himself; he laughed and spun round on his heel several times and how he shook and glided — round the rim of the fountain, on the grass, up and down the path; he had really got into the rhythm of it now and wouldn't stop though I could see he was getting more and more out of breath. Sometimes he danced in the light that came out of the drawingroom, sometimes he moved over into the dark and was illumined only by faint moonlight. But suddenly there was a third light, a great harsh beam that came from the Minister's car bringing him home from a late-night meeting. I hoped Biju would stop now but, on the contrary, he went on dancing right there in the driveway and only jumped out of the way before the advancing car at the last possible moment, and then he continued on the grass, at the same time saluting the Minister as he passed in the back-seat of the car. The Minister pretended not to see but seemed preoccupied with thoughts of the highest importance.

Sometimes Biju doesn't come for several days to the house. I don't miss him at all — on the contrary, I'm quite glad. I do all sorts of little things that I wouldn't do if he were there. For instance, I stick photographs of Mina into an album, or I tidy some drawers in the Minister's cupboard. I wait for them both to come home. Mina is there first. She talks to me about what she has been doing all day and about her friends. I do her hair in various attractive styles. She looks so nice, but when I have finished, she takes it all down again and plaits it back into a plain pigtail. I ask her whether she wouldn't like to get married but she laughs and says what for. I'm partly relieved but partly also worried because she is nearly twenty-two now. At one time she wanted to be a doctor but kept getting headaches on account of the hard studying she had to do, so she left it. I was glad. I never liked the idea of her becoming a doctor and having to work so hard and seeing so much suffering. The Minister was keen on it because he said the country needed a lot of doctors, but now he says what it needs even more is economists. So Mina often talks to me about becoming an economist.

On those days when Biju is not there, I seem to see more of the Minister. If he is late, I wait up for him to come. He is full of whatever he has been doing — whether attending a meeting or a dinner or some other function — and convinced that it was an event of great importance to the nation. Perhaps it was, I don't know. He tells me about it, and then it is like it was in the old days : I don't listen carefully but I'm glad to have him there. He still speaks with the same en- thusiasm and moves with the same energy while he is speaking, often bumping into things in his impatience. He continues to talk when we go up to bed and while he is undressing, but then he gets into bed and is suddenly fast asleep, almost in the middle of a sen- tence. I leave the light on for a while to look at him; I like to see him sleeping so peacefully, it makes me feel safe and comfortable.

When I get up next morning, I'm half hoping that Biju will not come that day either; but if there is no sign of him by afternoon, I get restless. I wonder what has happened. I telephone to his house, but his old servant is not much used to the telephone and it is difficult to understand or make him understand anything. In the end I have to go to Biju's house and see for myself. Usually there is nothing wrong with him and it is only one of his strange moods when he doesn't feel like getting out of bed or doing anything. After I have been with him for some time, he feels better and gets up and comes home with me. I'm glad to get him out of his house. It is not a cheerful place and he takes no care of it and his servant is too old to be able to keep it nicely. It is a rented house which he has taken only so that he can live in Delhi and be near us. It has cement floors, and broken-down servant quarters at the back, and no one ever looks after the garden so that when entering the gate one has to be careful not to get scratched by the thorny bushes that have grown all over the path.

Once I found him ill. He had a pain in his back and had not got up but kept lying there, not even allowing his bed to be made. It looked very crumpled and untidy and so did he, and this was strange and sad because when he is up he is always so very careful of himself. Now he was unshaven and his pyjama jacket was open, showing tangled grey hair growing on his chest. He looked at me with frightened eyes. I called the doctor, and then Biju was taken away to a nursing home, and he had to stay there for several weeks because they discovered he had a weak heart.

When he came out of the nursing home, the Minister wanted him to give up his house and come and live with us. But he wouldn't. It is strange about Biju : he has always gone where we have gone, but he has always taken a place on his own. He says that if he didn't live away from us, then where would he go every day and what would he do? I don't like to think of him alone at night in that house with only the old servant and with his violent dreams and his weak heart. The Minister too doesn't like it. Ever since he has heard about Biju's heart, he has been worried. And not only about Biju. He thinks of himself too, for he and Biju are about the same age, and he is afraid that anything that was wrong with Biju could be wrong with him too. In the days after Biju was taken to the nursing home, the Minister began not to feel well. He even woke up at nights and wanted me to put my hand on his heart. It felt perfectly all right to me, but he said no, it was beating too fast, and he was annoyed with me for not agreeing. He was convinced now that he too had a weak heart, so we called in the doctor and a cardiogram was taken and it was discovered that his heart was as healthy and sound as that of a fifteen-year-old boy. Then he was satisfied, and didn't have any more palpitations, and indeed forgot all about his heart.

I had an old aunt who was very religious. She was always saying her prayers and went to the temple to make her offerings. I was not religious at all. I never thought there is anything other than what there is every day. I didn't speak of these matters, and I don't speak of them today. I never like anyone to mention them to me. But my old aunt was always mentioning them, she could speak of nothing else. She said that even if I did not feel prayerful, I should at least go through the form of prayer, and if I only repeated the prescribed prayers every day, then slowly something would waken in my heart. But I wouldn't listen to her, and behind her back I laughed at her with Biju. He also did not believe in these things. Neither did the Minister, but whereas Biju and I only laughed and did not care about it much, the Minister made a great issue out of it and said a lot about religion retarding the progress of the people. He even told my aunt that for herself she could do what she liked, but he did not care for her to bring these superstitions into his house. She was shocked by all he said, and after that she never liked to stay with us, and when she did she avoided him as much as she could. She didn't avoid Biju and me, but continued to try and make us religious. One thing she said I have always remembered and sometimes I think about it. She said that yes, now it was easy for us not to care about religion, but later when our youth had gone, and our looks, and everything that gave us so much pleasure now had lost its savour, then what would we do, where would we turn?

Sometimes I too, like Biju, don't feel like getting up. Then I stay in bed with the curtains drawn all day. Mina comes in and is very concerned about me. She moves about the room and pulls at the curtains and rearranges things on my bedside table and settles my pillows and does everything she can to make me comfortable. She fully intends to stay with me all day, but after a while she gets restless. There are so many things for her to do and places to go to. She begins to telephone her friends and tells them that she can't meet them today because she is looking after her mother. I pretend to be very drowsy and ask why doesn't she go out while I'm asleep, it would be much better. At first she absolutely refuses, but after a while she says if I'm quite sure, and I urge her to go till at last she agrees. She gives me many hurried instructions as to rest and diet, and in saying goodbye she gathers me in her arms and embraces me so hard that I almost cry out. She leaves in a great hurry as if there was a lot of lost time to be made up. Then Biju comes in to sit with me. He reads the newspaper to himself, and when there is anything specially interesting he reads it aloud to me. He stays the whole day. Sometimes he dozes off in his chair, sometimes he lays cards out for patience. He is not at all bored or restless, but seems quite happy to stay not only for one day but for many more. I don't mind having him there; it is not very different from being by myself alone.

But when the Minister comes in, it is a great disturbance. "Why is it so dark in here?" he says and roughly pulls apart the curtains, dispelling the soothing honey-coloured light in which Biju and I have been all day like two fish in an aquarium. We both have to shut our eyes against the light coming in from the windows. My head begins to hurt; I suffer. "But what's the matter with you?" the Minister asks. He wants to call the doctor. He says when people are ill, naturally one calls a doctor. Biju asks "What will *he* do?" and this annoys the Minister. He gives Biju a lecture on modern science, and Biju defends himself by saying that not everything can be cured by science. As usual when they talk together for any length of time, the Minister gets more and more irritated with Biju. I can understand why. All the Minister's arguments are very sensible but Biju's aren't one bit sensible — in fact, after a while he stops answering altogether and instead begins to tear up the newspaper he has been reading and makes paper darts out of it. I watch him launching these darts. He looks very innocent while he is doing this, like a boy; he smiles to himself and his tie flutters over his shoulder. When people have a weak heart they can die quite suddenly, one has to expect it. I think of my old aunt asking where will you turn to? I look at the Minister. He too has begun to take an interest in Biju's paper darts. He picks one up and throws it into the air with a great swing of his body like a discus thrower; but it falls down on the carpet very lamely. He tries again and then again, always attempting this great sportsman's swing though not very successfully because he is so fat and heavy. It gives me pleasure to watch him; it also gives me pleasure to think of his strong heart like a fifteen-year-old boy's. There is a Persian poem. It says human life is like the petals that fall from the rose and lie soft and withering by the side of the vase. Whenever I think of this poem, I think of Biju and myself. But it is not possible to think of the Minister and Mina as rose petals. No, they are something much stronger. I'm glad! They are what I have to turn to, and it is enough for me. I need nothing more. My aunt was wrong.

*   *   *

A Course of English Studies

Nalini came from a very refined family. They were all great readers, and Nalini grew up on the classics. They were particularly fond of the English romantics, and of the great Russians. Sometimes they joked and said they were themselves like Chekhov characters. They were well off and lived gracious lives in a big house in Delhi, but they were always longing for the great capitals of Europe — London, Paris, Rome — where culture flourished and people were advanced and sophisticated.

Mummy and Daddy had travelled extensively in Europe in easier times (their honeymoon had been in Rome), and the boys had, one by one, been abroad for higher studies. At last it was Nalini's turn. She had finished her course in English literature at Delhi's exclusive Queen Alexandra College and now she was going to the fountainhead of it all, to England itself. She tried for several Universities, and finally got admission in a brand-new one in a Midland town. They were all happy about this, especially after someone told them that the new Universities were better than the old ones because of the more modern, go-ahead spirit that prevailed in them.

"Dearest Mummy, I'm sorry my last letters haven't been very cheerful but please don't get upset! Of course I love it here — who wouldn't! — and it was only because I was missing you darlings all so much that I sounded a bit miserable. Now that I know her better I can see Mrs. Crompton is a very nice lady, she is from a much better class than the usual type of landlady and I'm really lucky to be in her house. I have a reading list as long as my arm from classes! It's a stiff course but terribly exciting and I can hardly wait to get started on it all. The lecturers are very nice and the professor is a darling! Social and cultural activities have begun to be very hectic, there are so many societies to choose from it is difficult to know where to start. There are two music societies, one for classical music and the other for pop. You won't have to guess very hard which is the one I joined . . . "

Yes, there was the classical music society, and more, a poetry society, and the town had symphony concerts and a very good repertory company playing in a brand-new theatre financed by the Arts Council. It was a good place, full of cultural amenities and intelligent people, and the University was, as Nalini and her family had been told, modern and go-ahead, with a dynamic youngish Vice-Chancellor in charge. Nalini's letters home — she wrote three or four times a week — were full of everything that went on, and her mother lived it all with her. Sometimes, sitting in her drawingroom in Delhi on the yellow silk sofa, the mother, reading these letters, had tears in her eyes — tears of joy at the fullness and rapture of life and her own daughter a young girl at the very centre of it.

But Nalini was not as happy as she should have been. She did everything that she had always dreamed of doing, like going for walks in the English countryside and having long discussions over cups of coffee, but all the same something that she had expected, some flavour that had entered into her dreams, was not there. It was nothing to do with the weather. She had expected it to be bleak and raining, and she had spirits high enough to soar above that. She had also learned to adjust to her landlady, Mrs. Crompton, who had "moods" — as indeed it was her right to have for she had been the injured party in a divorce suit — and to be sympathetic when Mrs. Crompton did not feel up to cooking a hot meal. Of course, she missed Mummy and Daddy and the boys and the house and everything and everyone at home — *dreadfully*! — but it was the price she had been, and still was, willing to pay for the privilege of being in England. Besides, there was always the satisfaction of writing to them and as often hearing from them, and not only from them but from all the others too, her cousins and her college friends, with all of whom she was in constant correspondence. Every time the postman came, it was always with at least one letter for Nalini, so that Mrs. Crompton — who wasn't really expecting anything but nevertheless felt disappointed to have nothing — sometimes became quite snappish.

Nalini was not lonely in England. She got to know the people at college quite quickly, and even had her own group of special friends. These were all girls : they were friendly with the men students, and of course saw a lot of them during classes and the many extra-curricular activities, but special friendships were usually with members of one's own sex. So it was with a number or just a single girl friend that Nalini roamed over the college grounds, or sat in the canteen, or went to a concert, or out for a walk; and very pleasant and companionable it always was. Yet something was missing. She never wrote home about anything being missing so they all thought she was having as grand a time as her letters suggested. But she wasn't. Really, in spite of everything, all England at her disposal, she was disappointed.

One day she was out walking with her friend Maeve. They had left the town behind them and were walking down the lanes of an adjoining village. Sometimes these lanes were narrow and hemmed in by blackberry bushes that were still wet with water drops from recent rains; sometimes they opened up to disclose pale yellow fields, and pale green ones, and little hills, and brindled cows, and a pebbled church. The air was clear and moist. It was the English countryside of which the English poets — Shakespeare himself — had sung, and of which Mummy had so often spoken and tried to describe to Nalini. Maeve was talking about Anglo-Saxon vowel changes and the impossibility of remembering them; she was worried about this because there was a test coming up and she didn't know how she was ever going to get through it. Nalini also did not expect to get through, but quite other thoughts occupied her mind. Although she was fond of Maeve — who was a tall strong girl and looked like a big robin with her ruddy cheeks and brown coat and brown knitted stockings — Nalini could not help wishing that she was not there. She wanted to be alone, in order to give vent to the melancholy thoughts with which she felt oppressed. If she had been alone, perhaps she would have run through the fields, with the wind whipping her face; or she might have leaned her head against a tree, in which a thrush was singing, and sighed, and allowed the tears to flow down her cheeks.

The men students at the University were all very nice boys: eager and gentle and rather well-mannered in spite of the long hair and beards and rough shirts that so many of them affected. One could imagine a charming brother and sister relationship with them, and indeed that seemed to be what they themselves favoured when they went as far as establishing anything more personal with any of the girls. It would not have done for Nalini. She had enough brothers at home, and what she had (even if she didn't at the time know it) come to England for, what she expected from the place, what everything she had read had promised her, was love and a lover.

A girl in such a mood is rarely disappointed. One of the lecturers was Dr. Norman Greaves. He took the classes on Chaucer and his Age as well as on the Augustans, and although neither of these periods had ever been among Nalini's favourites, she began to attend the lectures on them with greater enthusiasm than any of the others. This was because Dr. Greaves had become her favourite teacher. At first she had liked the professor best — he was handsome, elegant, and often went up to London to take part in television programmes — but, after she had written her first essay for Dr. Greaves, she realised that it was he who was by far the finer person.

He had called her to his office and, tapping her essay with the back of his hand, said "This won't do, you know."

Nalini was used to such reactions from the lecturers after they had read her first essays. She could not, like the other English students, order her thoughts categorically, point by point, with discussion and lively development, but had to dash everything down, not thoughts but emotions, and moreover she could only do so in her own words, in the same way in which she wrote her letters home. But all the lecturers said that it wouldn't do, and when they said that, Nalini hung her head and didn't know what to answer. The others had just sighed and handed her essay back to her, but Dr. Greaves, after sighing, said "What are we going to do about you." He was really worried.

"I'll work harder, sir," Nalini promised.

"Yes well, that's nice of you," said Dr. Greaves, but he still looked worried and as if he thought her working harder wouldn't do all that much good. Nalini looked back at him, also worried; she bit her lip and her eyes were large. She feared he was going to say she wasn't good enough for the course.

" 'In *Troilus and Criseyde*,' " read Dr. Greaves, " 'Chaucer shows how well he knows the feelings in a woman's heart.' That's all right, but couldn't you be a bit more specific? What passages in particular did you have in mind?"

Nalini continued to stare at him; she was still biting her lip.

"Or didn't you have any in mind?"

"I don't know," she said miserably; and added — not, as far as she was concerned, at all inconsequentially — "I think I'm a very emotional sort of person."

He had given her essay back to her without any further comment; but there had been something in his manner as he did so which made her feel that a bad essay, though unfortunate, was not the end of the world. The others had not made her feel that way. Dr. Greaves soared above them all. He was not handsome like the professor, but she found much charm in him. He was rather short — which suited Nalini who was small herself — and thin, and exceptionally pale; his hair was pale too, and very straight and fine, of an indeterminate colour which may have been blond shading into grey. He was no longer young — in his thirties, at the end of his thirties indeed, perhaps even touching forty.

Nalini's life took on colour and excitement. She woke up early every morning and lay in bed wondering joyfully how many times she would see him that day. Tuesdays, Thursdays, and Fridays she was secure because those were days when he lectured; the other two days she was dependent on glimpses in corridors. These had the charm of sudden surprises, and there was always a sort of exquisite suspense as to what the next moment or the next corner turned might not reveal. But of course the best were lecture days. Then she could sit and look at him and watch and adore an hour at a time. He walked up and down the dais as he talked, and his pale hands fidgeted ceaselessly with the edges of his gown. His head was slightly to one side with the effort of concentration to get his thoughts across : he strove to be honest and clear on every point. His gown was old and full of chalk, and he always wore the same shabby tweed jacket and flannel trousers and striped college tie. He was not, unlike the professor and several others of the lecturers, a successful academic.

Weekends would have been empty and boring if she had not got into the habit of walking near his house. He lived on the outskirts of town in a Victorian house with a derelict garden. There had been several rows of these old houses, but most of them had been pulled down and replaced by new semi-detached villas which were sold on easy instalments to newly-weds. Dr. Greaves was not newly-wed; he had many children who ran all round the house and down the quiet lanes and out into the fields. These children were never very clean and their clothes were obviously handed down from one to the other. The babies of the young couples in the villas wore pink and blue nylon and were decorated with frills. All the young couples had shiny little cars but Dr. Greaves only had a bicycle.

One Saturday Nalini met him coming out of his house wheeling this bicycle. He was surprised to see her and wondered what she was doing there; and although she did not quite have the courage to tell him that she had been lingering around for him, neither did she stoop to tell him a lie. They walked together, he wheeling his bicycle. He called "Mervyn!" to a little boy who came dashing round a corner and was, to judge by his unkempt appearance, a son of his, but the boy took no notice and Dr. Greaves walked on patiently and as if he did not expect to have any notice taken.

It was a sunny day. Dr. Greaves was going into town on a shopping tour and Nalini accompanied him. They went into a supermarket and Dr. Greaves took a little wire basket and piled it up with a supply of washing soap and vinegar and sliced loaf and many other things which he read out from a list his wife had prepared for him. Nalini helped him find and take down everything from the shelves; sometimes she brought the wrong thing — a packet of dog biscuits

H

instead of baby rusks — and that made them laugh
quite a bit. Altogether it was fun; they were both
slow and inexpert and got into other people's way
and were grumbled at. Dr. Greaves was always very
apologetic to the people who grumbled, but Nalini
began to giggle. She giggled again at the cash desk
where he dropped some money and they had to
scrabble for it, while everybody waited and the cashier
clicked her tongue. Dr. Greaves went very pink and
kept saying, to the cashier and to the people whom he
kept waiting, "I'm most awfully sorry, do forgive me,
I am so sorry." Finally they got out of the shop and
he stood smiling at her, blinking his eyes against the
sun which was still shining, and thanked her for her
help. Then he rode away, rather slowly because of
the heavy load of shopping he had to carry from
the handlebars.

The next Saturday it was raining, but nevertheless
Nalini stood and waited for him outside his house.
At first he did not seem to be very pleased to see
her, and it was only when they had walked away
from the house for some distance, that he made her
sit on the cross-bar of his bicycle. They rode like
that together through the rain. It was like a dream,
she in his arms and feeling his breath on her face,
and everything around them, the trees and the sky
and the tops of the houses, melting away into mist
and soft rain. They went to the same shop and bought
almost the same things, but this time, when they came
out and she already saw the smile of farewell forming
on his lips, she quickly said "Can't we have coffee
somewhere?" They went to a shop which served home-
made rock cakes and had copper urns for decoration.

It was full of housewives having their coffee break, so the only table available was one by the coat rack, which was rather uncomfortable because of all the dripping coats and umbrellas. Nalini didn't mind, but Dr. Greaves sat hunched together and looking miserable. His thin hair was all wet and stuck to his head and sometimes a drop came dripping down his face. Nalini looked at him : "Cold?" she asked, with tender concern.

"How can you bear it here," he said. "In this dreadful climate." There was an edge to his voice, and his hand fidgeted irritably with the china ashtray.

"Oh I don't mind," said Nalini. "I've had so much sun all my life, it makes a change really." She smiled at him, and indeed as she did so, she radiated such warmth, such a sun all of her own, that he, who had looked up briefly, had at once to look down again as if it were too strong for him.

"And besides," she added after a short silence, "it's not what the weather is like outside that matters, but what you feel here, inside you." Her hand was pressed between her charming little breasts. Her eyes sought his.

"I hope," he said foolishly clearing his throat, "that you're happy in your work."

"Of course I am."

"Good. I thought your last essay showed some improvement, actually. Of course there's still a long way to go."

"I'll work hard, I promise!" she cried. "Only you see, I'm such a funny thing, oh dear, I simply can't learn anything, I'm stupid, my mind is like a stone — till I find someone who can *inspire* me. Now thank goodness," and she dropped her eyes and fidgeted with the other side of the ashtray, and then she raised her eyes again and she smiled, "I've found such a person." She continued to smile.

"You mean me," he said brusquely.

This put her off. She ceased to smile. She had expected more delicacy.

"My dear girl, I'm really not a fit person to inspire anyone. I'm just a hack, a work-horse. Don't expect anything from me. Oh my God, please," he said and held his head between his hands as if in pain, "don't look at me with those *eyes*."

"Are they so awfully ugly?"

"Leave me alone," he begged. "Let me be. I'm all right. I haven't complained, have I? I'm happy.

"No, you're not." She sagely shook her head. "I've read it in your face long ago. Why are these lines here," and she put out her finger and traced them, those lines of suffering running along the side of his mouth which she had studied over many lectures.

"Because I'm getting old. I'll be forty in May. *Forty*, mind you."

"Sometimes you look like a little boy. A little boy lost and I want to comfort him."

"Please let me go home now. I've got to buy fish and chips for Saturday lunch. They'll all be waiting."

"If you promise to meet me tomorrow. Promise? Norman?" She lightly touched his hand, and the look with which she met his was a teasing, victorious one as if she were challenging him to say no, if he could.

At home her landlady, Mrs. Crompton, was feeling unwell. She hadn't cooked anything and lay in bed in the dark, suffering. Nalini turned on the lights and the fires and went down in the kitchen and made scrambled eggs on toast. Then she carried a tray up to Mrs. Crompton's bedroom and sat on the side of Mrs. Crompton's bed and said "Oh you poor thing you," and stroked the red satin eiderdown. Mrs. Crompton sat up in bed in her bedjacket and ate the scrambled egg. She was a woman in early middle age and had a rather heavy, English face, with a strong nose and thin lips and a lowish forehead : it looked even heavier than usual because of the lines of disappointment and grief that seemed to pull it downwards. From time to time, as she ate, she sighed. Her bedroom was very attractively furnished, with ruffled curtains and bed-covers and a white rug, but it was sad on account of the empty twin bed which had been Mr. Crompton's and now just stood there parallel with Mrs. Crompton's, heavily eloquent under the bedcover which would never again be removed.

Nalini felt sorry for her and tried to cheer her up. She held one of Mrs. Crompton's large, cold hands in between her own small, brown, very warm ones and fondled it, and told her everything amusing that she could think of, like how she forgot her sari out on the washing line and it got soaking wet again in the rain, all six yards of it. Mrs. Crompton did not get cheered up much, her face remained long and gloomy, and at one point a tear could be seen slowly coursing its way along the side of her nose. Nalini watched its progress and suddenly, overcome with pity for the other's pain, she brought her face close to Mrs. Crompton's and kissed that dry, large-pored skin (how strange it felt! Nalini at once thought of Mummy's skin, velvet-smooth and smelling of almond oil) and as she did so, she murmured "Don't be sad;" she kept her face down on the pillow with Mrs. Crompton's and hidden against it, which was just as well, for although she really was so full of sympathy, none of this showed on her face which was blooming with joy.

"Dearest Mummy, Sorry sorry sorry! Yes you're right I've been awful about letters lately but if you knew how much work they pile on us! I've been working like a slave but it's fun. My favourites now are the Augustans. Yes darling, I know you're surprised and at first sight they do look cold like we've always said but they are very passionate underneath. I go out quite often into the country, it is so peaceful and beautiful. Sometimes it is windy and cold but it's funny, you know I always feel *hot*, everyone is surprised at it."

Norman usually wore a polo-neck sweater under his sports jacket, but Nalini never more than an embroidered shawl thrown lightly over her silk sari. Whenever they met, they went out into the country. They had found a place for themselves. It was a bus ride away from town, and when they got off the bus, they had to walk for about half a mile through some fields and finally through a lane which wound down into a small valley. Here there were four cottages, hidden away among trees and quite separate from each other. At the rear their gardens ran out into a little wood. The owners of the fourth and last cottage — a devoted old couple whom Norman had known and sometimes visited — had both died the year before and their cottage was for sale. At the bottom of its garden, just where the wood began, there was a little hut built, plank by loving plank, by the old dead owners themselves as a playroom for visiting grandchildren.

Now it served as a secret, hidden shelter for Norman and Nalini. No one ever came there — at most a cat or a squirrel scratching among the fallen leaves; and the loudest sounds were those of woodpeckers and, very occasionally, an aeroplane flying peacefully overhead. Nalini, who was really in these matters quite a practical girl, always brought all necessary things with her : light rugs and air cushions, packets of biscuits and sausage rolls. If it was cold and wet, they carpeted the hut with the rugs and stayed inside; on fine days, they sat in the wood with their backs leaning against the trunk of a tree and watching the squirrels.

Nalini loved picnics. She told Norman about the marvellous picnics they had at home, how the servants got the hampers ready and packed them in the back of the car, and then they drove off to some lovely spot — it might be a deserted palace, or an amphitheatre, or a summer tank, always some romantic ruin overgrown with creepers and flowers — and there rugs were spread for them and they lay on them and looked at the sky and talked of this and that, recited poetry and played jokes on each other; when the hampers were unpacked, they contained roast chickens, grapes, and chocolate cake.

"Yes," said Nalini, "it was lovely but this," she said and ate a dry Marie biscuit, "this is a million billion times better."

She meant it. He lay beside her on the rug they had spread; it was a fine day, so they were under a tree. Dead leaves crunched under the rug every time they moved; there weren't many left up on the branches, and some of them were bright red and hung in precarious isolation on their stalks.

Norman too sighed with contentment. "Tell me more," he said. He never tired of hearing about her family life in their house in Delhi or, in the summer, up in Simla.

"But you've heard it all hundreds of times! Tell me about you now. You never tell me anything."

"Oh me," said Norman. "My life's tended to be rather dowdy up till now."

"And now?"

He groaned with excess of feeling and gathered her into his arms. He kissed her shoulder, her neck, one temple; he murmured from out of her hair "You smell of honey."

"Do you think of me when I'm not there?"

"Constantly."

"When you're lecturing?"

"Yes."

"When you're with your wife?"

He released her, and lay down again, and shut his eyes. She bent close over him; her coil of hair had come half undone and she made it brush against his cheek. "Tell me how you think of me," she said.

"As a vision and a glory," he said without opening his eyes. She drank in his face : how fine it looked, the skin thin and pale as paper with a multitude of delicate lines traced along the forehead, and the two deeply engraved lines that ran from his nose to his lips. It was a face, she felt, designed to register only the highest emotions known to mankind.

"What sort of a vision?" she asked. And when he didn't answer, she begged him "I want to hear it from you, tell me in beautiful words."

He smiled at that and sat up and kissed her again;

he said "There aren't any words beautiful enough."

"Oh yes, yes! Think of Chaucer and Pope! Do you ever write poetry, Norman? You don't have to tell me — I know you do. You're a poet really, aren't you? At heart you are."

"I haven't written anything in years."

"But now you'll start again, I know it."

He smiled and said "It's too late to start anything again."

But she would never let him talk like that. If he referred to his forty years, his family, the moderateness of his fortunes, she would brush him aside and say that from now on everything would be different. She did not say how it would be different, nor did she think about it much; but she saw grand vistas opening before them both. Certainly it was inconceivable that, after the grand feelings that had caught them up, anything could ever be the same for either of them again. For the time being, however, she was content to let things go on as they were. She would be here for another two years, finishing her course; and although of course it would have been marvellous if they could have lived together in the same house, since that could not be, she would carry on with Mrs. Crompton and he with his family. When the two years were up, they would see. Meanwhile, they had their hut and one another's hearts — what else mattered? She was perfectly happy and wanted, for the moment, nothing more.

It was he who was restless and worried. She noticed during lectures that his hands played even more nervously with the edges of his gown than before; his face looked drawn, and quite often nowadays he seemed to have cut himself shaving so that the pallor of his cheeks was enhanced by a little blob of dried blood. Once in her anxiety she even approached him after lectures and, under cover of asking some academic question, whispered "Is something wrong? Are you ill?" A frightened expression came into his eyes.

Afterwards, when they were alone together in their own place, he begged her never again to talk to him like that in class. She laughed : "What's it matter? No one noticed."

"I don't care if they noticed or not. I don't want it. It simply frightens me to death."

"You're so timid," she teased him, "like a little mouse."

"That's true. I always have been. All my life I've been terrified of being found out."

At that she tossed her head. She certainly had no such fears and did not ever expect to have them.

Then he said, "I rather think I *have* been found out;" and added "It's Estelle."

"Have you told her?"

"When you've been married to someone as long as that, they don't need to be told anything."

After a short pause, she said "I'm glad. Now everything is in the open."

She knew certain steps would have to be taken, but was not sure what they were. It was no use consulting with Norman, he was in no state to plan anything; and besides, she wanted to spare him all the anxiety she could. In previous dilemmas of her life, she had always had Mummy by her side, and how they would discuss and talk and weigh the pros and cons, sitting up in Mummy's large, cool bedroom with the airconditioner on. Now Mummy was not there, and even if she had been, this was a matter on which she would not be able to give advice. Poor Mummy, Nalini thought affectionately, how restricted her life had always been, how set in its pattern of being married and having children and growing older, and tasting life only through books and dreams.

Her English friends at college were also not fit to be let into an affair of such magnitude. Nalini was fond of them, of Maeve and the rest, but she could no longer take them quite seriously. This was because they were not serious people. Their concerns were of a superficial order, and even when they had connections with the men students, these too remained on a superficial level; never, at any point, did their lives seem to touch those depths of human involvement where Nalini now had her being. Once she had a long heart-to-heart talk with Maeve. Actually, it was Maeve who did most of the talking. They were in her room, which was very cosy, with a studio couch and an orange-shaded lamp and an open fire in the grate. They sat on the floor by the fire and drank coffee out of pottery mugs. Maeve talked of the future, how she hoped to get a research studentship and write a thesis on the political pamphlets of the early eighteenth century; for this she would have to go to London and spend a lot of time in the British Museum Reading Room. She spoke about all this very slowly and seriously, sitting on the floor with her long legs in brown knitted stockings stretched out in front of her and her head leaned back to rest against a chair; she blew smoke from her cigarette with a thoughtful air. Nalini had her legs tucked under her, which came easily to her, and her sari billowed around her in pale blue silk; sometimes she put up her hand to arrange something — her hair, a fold of her sari — and then the gold bangles jingled on her arms. There was something almost frivolous in her presence in that room with all the books and the desk full of notes and Maeve's favourite Henry Moore study on the wall. Yet it wasn't Nalini who was frivolous, it was large, solid Maeve. How could anyone, thought Nalini, endeavouring to listen with a sympathetic expression to what her friend was saying, talk with so serious an air of so unserious a future — indeed, how could a future spent in the British Museum Reading Room be considered as a future at all? She pitied Maeve, who looked healthy and human enough with her bright red cheeks and her long brown hair, but who did not appear to have as much as an inkling of what riches, what potentialities, lay waiting within a woman's span of life.

Mrs. Crompton seemed to know more about it. She carried, at any rate, a sense of loss, the obverse side of which postulated a sense of possibilities : she knew a woman's sorrow and so· must have, Nalini inferred, some notion of a woman's joy. Mrs. Crompton was not an easy person to get along with. She was hard and autocratic, and ran her household with an iron discipline. Every single little thing had its place, every action of the day its time : no kettle to be put on between ten in the morning and five in the afternoon, no radio to be switched on before noon. She did not encourage telephone calls. Nalini, who at home was used to a luxuriantly relaxed way of life, did not, after the initial shock, find it too difficult to fall in with Mrs. Crompton's rigid regime and always did her best to humour her. As a result, Mrs. Crompton trusted her, even perhaps liked her as far as she was capable of liking (which was not, on the whole, very far — she was not by nature an affectionate person). They spent quite a lot of their evenings together, which suited both of them for, strangely enough, Nalini discovered that she was beginning to prefer Mrs. Crompton's company to that of the girls at college.

Indeed, in the evenings Mrs. Crompton became a somewhat different person. When the day was done and its duties fulfilled, when the curtains were drawn and chairs arranged closer to the fire, at this cosy domestic hour her normally stern daytime manner began if not to crumble then at any rate to soften. Memories surged up in her, memories of Mr. Crompton — though not so much of their life together as of their final parting. This seemed to have been the event in her life which stirred her deeper than anything that had ever gone before or come after. It had played, and was still playing, all her chords and made her reverbate with feelings of tremendous strength. Nalini admired these feelings : it was living, it was passion, it was the way a woman should be. She never tired of listening to Mrs. Crompton's story, she was the unfailing attendant and sympathiser of the tears that were wrung from this strong person. Nalini heard not only about Mr. Crompton but also, a lot, about the other woman who had taken him away. There was one incident especially that Mrs. Crompton often rehearsed and that Nalini listened to with special interest. It was when the other woman had come to visit Mrs. Crompton (quite unexpectedly, one morning while she was hoovering in the back bedroom) and had asked her to

give Mr. Crompton up. Mrs. Crompton had been at a
disadvantage because she was only in her housedress
and a turban tied round her head while the other
woman had had her hair newly done and was in a
smart red suit with matching bag and shoes; nevertheless Mrs. Crompton had managed to carry off the
occasion with such dignity — without showing anger,
without even once raising her voice, doing nothing
more in fact than in a firm voice enunciating right
principles — that it was the other woman who had wept
and, before leaving, had had to go to the bathroom to
repair her make-up.

Nalini was careful to wear her plainest sari when she
went to call on Estelle Greaves. She had no desire to
show Norman's wife up to an even greater disadvantage
than she guessed she already would be. She had not,
however, expected to find quite so unattractive a
person. She was shocked, and afterwards kept asking
Norman : "But how did you ever get married to her?"

Norman didn't answer. There were dark patches of
shadow under his eyes, and he kept running his hand
through his hair.

"She can't ever have been pretty. It's not possible,
how can she? Of course, probably she wasn't so fat
before but even so — *and* she's older than you."

"She's the same age."

"She looks years older."

"For God's sake," Norman said suddenly, "shut up."

Nalini was surprised, but she saw it was best to
humour him. And it was such a beautiful day, they
ought really to be doing nothing but enjoy it. There
was a winter stillness in the air, and a hint of ice in
its sharp crystal clearness against which the touches of

autumn that still lingered in fields, trees, and hedges looked flushed and exotic. "Let's walk a bit," she said, tucking her hand under his arm.

He disengaged himself from her : "Why did you do it?" he said in a puzzled, tortured way. "Whatever possessed you?"

"I wanted to clear the air," she said grandly; and added, even more grandly, "I can't live with a lie."

He gave a shout of exasperation; then he asked "Is that the sort of language you used with her?"

"Oh, with her." Nalini shrugged and pouted. "She's just impossible to talk to. Whenever you try and start on anything serious with her, she jumps up and says the shepherd's pie is burning. Oh Norman, Norman, how do you stand it? How can you live with her and in such an atmosphere? Your house is so — I don't know, uncared for. Everything needs cleaning and repairing. I can't bear to think of you in such a place, you with your love for literature and everything that's lovely —"

He winced and walked away from her. He did not walk through the wood but along the edge of it, in the direction of the next house. This was a way they usually avoided, for they wanted to steer clear of the old people living around. But today he seemed too distraught to care.

"Why are you annoyed with me?" she asked, following him. "I did right, Norman."

"No," he said; he stopped still and looked at her, earnestly, in pain : "You did very, very wrong."

She touched his pale cheek, pleadingly. Her hand was frail and so was her wrist round which she wore three gold bangles. Suddenly he seized her hand and

kissed its palm many times over. They went back to
their hut where they bolted the door, and at once he
was making love to her with the same desperate fever-
ishness with which he had kissed her hand.

She was well pleased, but he more guilty and downcast than before. As he fastened his clothes, he said
"You know, I really mustn't see you any more."

She laughed : "Silly Billy," she said, tenderly, gaily,
in her soft Indian accent.

But from this time on, he often declared that it was
time they parted. He blamed himself for coming to
meet her at all and said that, if he had any resolution
in him, he would not show up again. She was not
disturbed by these threats — which she knew perfectly
well he could never carry out — but sometimes they
irritated her.

She told him "It's your wife who's putting you up
to this." He looked at her for a moment as if she were
mad. "She hates me," Nalini said.

"She hasn't said so. But of course you can't
expect —"

"Well I hate her too," Nalini said. "She is stupid."

"No one could call Estelle stupid."

"I've met her, so you can't tell me. She has nothing
to say and she doesn't even understand what's said to
her. It's impossible to talk to her intelligently."

"What did you expect her to talk to you intelligently
about?"

"About you. Us. Everything.

He was silent, so she assumed she had won her
point. She began to do her hair. She took out all her
pins and gave them to him to hold. But it turned out
that he had more to say.

"It was so wrong of you to come to our house like that. And what did you want? Some great seething scene of passion and renunciation, such as Indians like to indulge in?"

"Don't dare say anything bad against my country!"

"I'm not, for God's sake, saying anything bad against your country!"

"Yes, you are. And it's your wife who has taught you. I could see at one glance that she was anti-Indian."

"Please don't let's talk about my wife any more."

"Yes, we will talk about her. I'll talk about her as much as I like. What do you think, I'm some fallen woman that I'm not allowed to speak your wife's name? Give me my pins." She plucked them from out of his hand and stabbed them angrily into her coil of hair. "And I'll tell you something more. From now on everything is going to change. I'm tired of this hole and corner business. You must get a divorce."

"A splendid idea. You're not forgetting that I have four children?"

"You can have ten for all I care. You must leave that woman! It is she or I. Choose."

Norman got up and let himself out of the hut. At the door he turned and said in a quiet voice "You know I'm no good at these grand scenes."

He walked away through the garden up on to the path which would lead him to the bus-stop. He had a small, lithe figure and walked with his head erect, showing some dignity; he did not look back nor lose that dignity even when she shouted after him : "You're afraid! You're a coward! You want to have your cake and eat it!"

They made it up after a day or two. But their

I

separate ideas remained, his that they must part, hers that he must get a divorce. They began to quarrel quite frequently. She enjoyed these fights, both for themselves and for the lovely sensations involved in making them up afterwards. He found them exasperating, and called her a harridan and a fishwife : a preposterous appellation, for what could be further from the image of a harridan and a fishwife than this delicate little creature in silk and gold, with the soft voice and the soft, tender ways. Once he asked her : "All right — supposing I get a divorce, what next? What do you suggest? Do we stay here, do I go on teaching at the University and support two families on my princely salary? You tell me."

"Oh no," she said at once, "I'll take you with me to India."

This idea amused him immensely. He saw himself taken away as a white slave-boy, cozened and coddled and taught to play the flute. He asked her to describe how they would live in India, and she said that she would dress him up in a silk pyjama and she would oil his hair and curl it round her finger and twice a day, morning and evening, she would bathe him in milk. It became one of their pastimes to play at being in India, a game in which he would loll on the rug spread on the floor of their hut and she would hold his head in her lap and comb him and pet him and massage his cheeks : this was fun, but it did not, Nalini reflected, get them any further.

"Dearest Mummy, How I long for one of our cosy chats up in the bedroom. I have so much to tell you. Darling Mummy, I have found someone with whom I want to share my life and I know you too will love him. He is exactly the sort of person we have always dreamed of, so sensitive and intelligent like an English poet." But she never sent that letter. Mummy was so far away, it might be difficult for her to understand. Besides, she could not really do anything yet to solve their practical problems. One of these was particularly pressing just now. Winter had come on, and it was beginning to get too cold to use their hut. Icy blasts penetrated through the wooden boards, and Norman's teeth never stopped chattering. But where else could they go? Norman said nowhere, it just meant that they must not see each other any more, that the cycle of seasons was dictating what moral right had already insisted on long ago. Nalini had learned to ignore such defeatist talk.

It was around this time that she first confided in Mrs. Crompton. This came about quite naturally, one evening when they were both sitting by the fire, Mrs. Crompton with her large hands in her lap, Nalini crocheting a little rose bedjacket for herself. Sometimes Nalini lowered her work and stared before her with tragic eyes. It was silent in the room, with a low hum from the electric fire. Nalini sighed, and Mrs. Crompton sighed, and then Nalini sighed again. Words were waiting to be spoken, and before long they were. Nalini told her everything : about Norman, and Estelle, and the children, and the hut, and the cold weather. Also how Norman was going to get a divorce and go away with her to India. Mrs. Crompton listened without comment but with, it seemed, sympathy. Later, when they had already said goodnight and Nalini had gone up to her room and changed into her brushed nylon nightie, Mrs. Crompton came in to tell her that it would be all right if she brought Norman to the house. Nalini gave a big whoop and flung her arms round Mrs. Crompton's neck, just as she used to do to Mummy when Mummy had done something lovely and nice, crying in a voice chock-full of gratitude, "Oh you darling, you darling you!"

Norman hated coming to the house. He kept saying he was sure Mrs. Crompton was listening outside the door. Once Nalini abruptly opened the door of her room, to convince him that no one was there, but he only shook his head and said that she was listening through the ceiling from downstairs. Certainly, they were both of them — even Nalini — very much aware of Mrs. Crompton's presence in the house. Sometimes they heard her moving about and that put them out, and sometimes they didn't hear any sound from her at all and that put them out even more. When it was time for Norman to leave and they came down the stairs, she was invariably there, waiting for them in the hall. "Do have a cup of tea before you go," she would say, but he always made some excuse and left hurriedly. Then she would be disappointed, even a little surly, and Nalini would have to work hard to soothe her.

Nalini had made her room so attractive with lots of photographs of the family and embroidered cushions and an Indian wall-hanging, but Norman was always uncomfortable, all the time he was there. Sometimes even he would make an excuse not to come, he would send a note to say he had a lecture to deliver at an evening class, or that he was suffering from toothache and had to visit the dentist. Then Mrs. Crompton and Nalini would both be disappointed and turn off the lights and the fires and go to bed early.

She boldly went up to him after classes and said "You haven't been for a *week*." He raised his eyes — which were a very pale, almost translucent blue, and remarkably clear amid the dark shadows left around them by anxiety and sleepless nights — and he looked with them not at her but directly over her head. But he came that evening. He said "I told you you mustn't ever do that."

"I had to — you didn't come so long."

He sighed and passed his hand over his eyes and down his face.

"You're tired," she said. "My poor darling, you've been working too hard." With swift, graceful movements, which set her bangles jingling, she settled pillows on her bed and smoothed the counterpane invitingly. But he didn't lie down. He hadn't even taken his coat off.

"Please let me go, Nalini," he said in a quiet, grave voice.

"Go where, my own darling?"

"I want us not to see each other any more."

"Again!"

"No, this time really — please." He sank into an armchair, as if in utter exhaustion.

"You've been talking to your wife," she said accusingly.

"Who would I talk to if not to my wife. She *is* my wife, you know, Nalini. We've been together for a long time and through all sorts of things. That does mean a lot. I'm a wretchedly weak person and you must forgive me."

"You're not weak. You're sensitive. Like an artist."

He made a helpless, hopeless gesture with his hand.

Then he got up and quickly went downstairs. Mrs. Crompton was waiting at the foot of the stairs. She said "Do have a cup of tea before you go." Norman didn't answer but hurried away. He had his coat collar up and there was something guilty and suspicious about him which made Mrs. Crompton look after him with narrowed eyes.

Mrs. Crompton told Nalini about men : that they were selfish and grasping and took what they wanted, and then they left. She illustrated all this with reference to Mr. Crompton. But Nalini did not believe that Norman was like Mr. Crompton. Norman was suffering. She could hardly bear to look at him during lectures because she saw how he suffered. These were terrible days. It was the end of winter, and whatever snow there had been, was now melting and the same slush colour as the sky that drooped spiritlessly over the town. Nalini felt the cold at last, and wore heavy sweaters and coats over her sari, and boots on her small feet. She hated being muffled up like that and sometimes she felt she was choking. She didn't know what to do with herself nowadays — she did not care to be much with the girls at college and she had lost the taste for Mrs. Crompton's company. She hardly worked at all and got very low marks in all her subjects. Once the professor called her and told her that she would either have to do better or leave the course. She burst into tears and he thought it was because of what he was saying, but it wasn't that at all : she often cried nowadays, tears spurting out of her eyes at unexpected moments. She spent a lot of time in bed, crying. She tossed from side to side, thinking, wondering. She could not understand how it could all have ended like that, so abruptly and for nothing. They had been happy, and it had been radiant and wonderful, and after that how could he go back to that house with the leaking taps and the ungainly woman in it and all those children?

The weather was warmer. It was a good spring that year, and crocuses appeared even in Mrs. Crompton's garden. Nalini began to feel better — not happy, but better. She went out for walks again with one or two friends, and sometimes they had tea together, or went to the music society. It was all very much like before. One fine Sunday she and Maeve took a walk outside the town. There were cows in the fields, and newly-shorn sheep, and the hedges were brimming with tiny buds. Nalini remembered how she had walked with Maeve the year before, and how dissatisfied she had felt while Maeve, in her brown knitted stockings, talked of Anglo-Saxon vowel changes. Today Maeve wore patterned stockings, and she talked of her chances of a research studentship; there were several other strong candidates in the field — for instance, Dorothy Horne whose forte was the metaphysicals. Nalini listened to her with kindly interest. The air was full of balmy scents and the sky of little white clouds like lambs. Nalini felt sorry for Maeve and, after that, she felt sorry for all of them — Dorothy Horne and the other girls, and Mrs. Crompton and Norman.

"Dearest Mummy, What a clever clever little thing you are! Yes you are right, I have not been happy lately . . . You know me so well, our hearts are open to each other even with such a distance between us. Here people are not like that. I don't believe that Shakespeare or Keats or Shelley or any of them can have been English! I think they were Indians, at least in their previous birth!!! Darling, please talk to Daddy and ask him to let me come home for the long vac. I miss you and long for you and want to be with you all soon. I don't think the teaching here is all that good, there is no one like Miss Subramaniam at the dear old Queen Alex with such genuine love for literature and able to inspire their pupils. A thousand million billion kisses, my angel Mummy."

*   *   *

The Housewife

She had her music lesson very early in the morning before anyone else was awake. She had it up on the roof of the house so no one was disturbed. By the time the others were up, she had already cooked the morning meal and was supervising the cleaning of the house. She spent the rest of the day in seeing to the family and doing whatever had to be done, so no one could say that her music in any way interfered with her household duties. Her husband certainly had no complaints. He wasn't interested in her singing but indulged her in it because he knew it gave her pleasure. When his old aunt, Phuphiji, who lived with them, hinted that it wasn't seemly for a housewife, a matron like Shakuntala, to take singing lessons, he ignored her. He was good at ignoring female relatives, he had had a lot of practice at it. But he never ignored Shakuntala. They had been married for twenty-five years and he loved her more year by year.

It wasn't because of anything Phuphiji said but because of him, who said nothing, that Shakuntala sometimes felt guilty. And because of her daughter and her little grandson. She loved all of them, but she could not deny to herself that her singing meant even more to her than her feelings as wife and mother and grandmother. She was unable to explain this, she tried not to think of it. But it was true that with her music she lived in a region where she felt most truly, most deeply herself. No, not herself, something more and higher than that. By contrast with her singing, the rest of her day, indeed of her life, seemed insignificant. She felt this to be wrong but there was no point in trying to struggle against it. Without her hour's practice in the morning, she was as if deprived of food and water and air.

One day her teacher did not come. She went on the roof and practised by herself but it was not the same thing. By herself she felt weak and faltering. She *was* weak and faltering, but when he was there it didn't matter so much because he had such strength. Later, when her husband had gone to his place of work (he was a building contractor) and she had arranged everything for the day's meals and left Phuphiji entertaining some friends from the neighbourhood with tea, she went to find out what had happened. She took her servant-boy with her to show her the way, for although she often sent messages to her teacher's house, she had not been there before. The house was old and in a narrow old alley. There was some sort of workshop downstairs and she had to step over straw and bits of packing-cases; on the first floor was a music school consisting of a long room in which several people sat on the floor playing on drums. Her teacher lived on the second storey. He had only one room and everything was in great disorder. There was practically no furniture but a great many discarded clothes were hung up on hooks and on a line strung across the room. A bedraggled, cross woman sat on the floor, turning the handle of a sewing-machine. The teacher himself lay on a mat in a corner, tossing and groaning; when Shakuntala, full of concern, bent over him, he opened his eyes and said "I'm going now." He wore a red cloth tied round his brow and this gave him a rather gruesome appearance.

Shakuntala tried to rally him, but the more she did so, the sicker he became. "No," he insisted, "I'm going." Then he added "I'm not afraid to die."

His wife, turning the handle of her sewing-machine, snorted derisively. This did rally him; he gathered sufficient strength to prop himself up on one elbow. "There's no food," he said to Shakuntala, making pathetic gestures towards his mouth to show how he lacked sustenance to put into it. "She doesn't know how to cook for a sick person."

His wife stopped sewing in order to laugh heartily. "Soup!" she laughed. "That's what he's asking for. Where has he ever tasted soup? In his father's house? They thought themselves lucky if they could get a bit of dal with their dry bread. *Soup*," she repeated in a shaking voice, her amusement abruptly changing into anger.

Shakuntala, who had not anticipated being caught in a domestic quarrel, was embarrassed. But she also felt sorry for the teacher. She did not believe him to be very ill but she saw he was very uncomfortable. The room was hot, and dense with various smells, and full of flies; there was thumping from the workshop downstairs, drums and some thin stringed instruments from the music school, and inside the room the angry whirring of the sewing-machine. In spite of the heat, the sick man was covered with a sheet under which he tossed and turned — not with pain, Shakuntala saw, but with irritation.

After that her own home seemed so sweet and orderly to her. They had recently built a new bungalow with shiny woodwork and pink and green terrazzo floors. Their drawingroom was furnished with a blue rexine-covered sofa-set. She wished she could have brought her teacher here to nurse him; she could have made him so comfortable. All day she was restless, thinking of that. And as always when Shakuntala was restless and her mind turned away from her household affairs, Phuphiji noticed and pursued her through the house and insisted on drawing her attention to various deficiencies such as the month's sugar supply running out too quickly or a cooking vessel not having been scoured to shine as it should. Shakuntala had lived with Phuphiji long enough to remain calm and answer her calmly, but Phuphiji had also lived with Shakuntala long enough to know that these answers were desultory and that Shakuntala's thoughts remained fixed elsewhere. She continued to follow her, to circle her, to fix her with her bright old eyes.

Later in the day Shakuntala's daughter Manju came with little Baba. Of course Shakuntala was happy to see them and played with and kissed Baba as usual; but, like Phuphiji, Manju noticed her mother's distraction. Manju became querulous and had many complaints. She said she had a headache every morning, and Baba sometimes was very naughty and woke them all up in the night and wanted to play. For all this she required her mother's sympathy, and Shakuntala gave it but Manju noticed that she couldn't give it with all her heart and that made her more querulous. And Phuphiji joined in, encouraging Manju, pitying her, drawing the subject out more and more and all the time keeping her eyes on Shakuntala to make sure she participated as keenly as she was in duty bound to. Between them, they drove Shakuntala quite crazy;

and the worst of it was that she was on their side, she knew that she ought to be absorbed in their problems and blamed herself because she wasn't.

It was a relief to her when her husband came home, for he was the one person who was always satisfied with her. Unlike the others, he wasn't interested in her secret thoughts. For him it was enough that she dressed up nicely before his arrival home and oiled her hair and adorned it with a wreath of jasmine. She was in her early forties but plump and fresh. She loved jewellery and always wore great quantities of it, even in the house. Her arms were full of bangles, she had a diamond nose-ring and a gold necklace round her smooth, soft neck. Her husband liked to see all that; and he liked her to stand beside him to serve him his meal, and then to lie next to him on the bed while he slept. That night he fell asleep as usual after eating large helpings of food. He slept fast and sound, breathing loudly for he was a big man with a lot of weight on him. Sometimes he tossed himself from one side to the other with a grunt. Then Shakuntala gently patted him as if to soothe him; she wanted him to be always entirely comfortable and recognised it to be her mission in life to see that he was. When she fell asleep herself, she slept badly and was disturbed by garbled dreams.

But the next morning the teacher was there again. He wasn't ill at all any more, and when she enquired after his health, he shrugged as if he had forgotten there had ever been anything wrong with it. She sang so well that day that even he was satisfied — at least he didn't make the sour face he usually wore while listening to her. As she sang, her irritation and anxiety dissolved and she felt entirely clear and happy. The sky was translucent with dawn and birds woke up and twittered like fresh gurgling water. No one else was up in the whole neighbourhood, only she and the teacher and the birds. She sang and sang, her voice rose high and so did her heart; sometimes she laughed with enjoyment and saw that in response the shadow of a smile flitted over the teacher's features as well. Then she laughed again and her voice rose — with what ease — to even greater feats. And the joy that filled her at her own achievement and the peace that entered into her with that pure clear dawn, these sensations stayed with her for the rest of the day. She polished all the mirrors and brass fittings with her own hands, and afterwards she cooked sweet vermicelli for her husband which was his favourite dish. Phuphiji, at once aware of her change of mood, was suspicious and followed her around as she had done the previous day and looked at her in the same suspicious way; but today Shakuntala didn't mind, in fact she even laughed at Phuphiji within herself.

Her teacher always went away after the early morning lesson, but about this time, after his illness, he began to visit her in the afternoons as well. Shakuntala was glad. Now that she had seen his home, she realised what a relief it must be to him to have a clean and peaceful room to sit in; and she did her best to make him comfortable and served him with tea and little fried delicacies. But he was never keen on these refreshments and often did not touch anything she set before him, simply letting his eyes glance over it with the expression of distaste that was so

characteristic of him. Phuphiji was amazed. She
thought he was being excessively and unwarrantably
honoured by having these treats placed before him
and could not understand why he did not fall upon
them as eagerly as she expected him to. She looked
from them to him and back again. Tantalised beyond
endurance, she even pushed the dishes towards him,
saying "Eat, eat," as if he were some bizarre animal
whose feeding habits she wished to observe. He
treated her in the same way as he did the refreshments, ignoring her after a swift contemptuous glance
in her direction. But she was fascinated by him. Whenever he came, she hurried and placed herself in a
strategic position in order to look her fill into his
face. Sometimes as she gazed she shook her head in
wonder and murmured to herself and even gave herself incredulous little laughs. He wasn't bothered by
her in the least. He sat there for as long as he felt
like it, often in complete silence, and then departed,
still in silence.

Occasionally, however, he talked. His conversation
was as arbitrary as his silence; he needed no stimulus
to start him off and always ended as abruptly as he
had begun. Shakuntala loved listening to him, everything he said was of interest to her. She was especially
fascinated when he talked about his own teacher who
had been a very great and famous and temperamental
musician. He often spoke of him, for a good many
years of his life and certainly the most formative part
of it had been spent under the old man's tutelage.
All the disciples had lived with their guru and his
family in an old house in Benaras. There had been
strict discipline as far as the hours of practice were

concerned and all were expected to get up before
dawn and spend most of their day in improving their
technique; but in between their way of life was entirely
without constraint. They ate when they liked, slept
when they liked, chewed opium in their betel, loved
and formed friendships. When the old man was invited to perform at private or public concerts in other
parts of India, most of the disciples travelled with
him. They all crammed together into a railway carriage,
and when they got to their destination, they stayed
together in the quarters allotted to them. Sometimes
these were a dingy room in a rest-house, other times
they were ornate chambers in some Maharaja's palace.
They were equally happy wherever it was, sleeping on
the floor round the great bed on which their guru
snored, and eating their fill of the rich meals provided
for them. They were up all night listening to and
performing in concerts that never ended before dawn.
They were most of them quite unattached and had
no ties apart from those they had formed with their
guru. Some of them — such as Shakuntala's teacher —
had run away from their parents to be with their
guru, others had left their wives and children for his
sake. He was a very hard master. He often beat his
disciples, and they had to serve him as his servants,
doing the most menial tasks for him; he never lifted
a finger for himself and got into a terrible rage if
some little comfort of his had been neglected. Once
Shakuntala's teacher had forgotten to light his hookah,
and for this fault was chased all round the house and
at last out into the street where he had to stay for
three days, sitting on the doorstep like a beggar and
being fed on scraps till he was forgiven and admitted

inside again. Phuphiji was shocked to hear of such treatment and called the guru by many harsh names; but to Shakuntala, as to her teacher, it did not seem so deplorable — on the contrary, she thought it a reasonable price to pay for the privilege of being near so great and blessed a man.

Whenever a famous musician came to the town to give a performance, Shakuntala did her best to attend. It was not easy for her because she had no one willingly to go with her. She didn't want to trouble her husband. He cared nothing for music and, in any case, would have found it an ordeal to sit upright on a chair for so many hours. Once or twice she asked Phuphiji to be her chaperone. Phuphiji was quite glad, she always enjoyed an outing. At first she was interested in everything, she looked round eagerly, craning her neck this way and that. But when the concert started and went on, she became restless. She yawned and slid about on the chair to show how uncomfortable she was; she asked often how much longer they would have to stay, and then she said "Let's go," and when Shakuntala tried to soothe and detain her, she became plaintive and said her back was hurting unbearably. So they always had to come home early, just as the best part of the concert was beginning. And it wasn't much better when Shakuntala took her daughter with her, for although Manju didn't complain the way Phuphiji did, she was obviously bored and made a suffering face. It was usually necessary to take Baba along too, and if they were lucky, he fell asleep quite soon, but if they weren't, he made a lot of disturbance and

K

kicked and struggled and finally he would begin to
cry so that there was nothing for it, they had to
leave. Shakuntala always tried to put a good face on
it and hide her disappointment, but later, when she
was at home and in bed beside her husband who
had been asleep these many hours, then her thoughts
kept reverting to the concert. She wondered what
raga was being sung now — Raga Yaman, serene and
sublime, Raga Kalawati, full of sweet yearning? —
and saw the brightly lit stage on which the musicians sat: the singer in the middle, the accompanists
grouped all round, the disciples forming an outer ring,
and all of them caught up in a mood of exaltation
inspired by the music. Their heads slowly swayed,
they exchanged looks and smiles, their hearts were
open and sweet sensations flowed in them like honey.
And thinking of this, alone in the silent bedroom
beside her sleeping husband, she turned her face and
buried it deep into her pillow as if she hoped thereby
to bury her feelings of bitter disappointment.

One morning her teacher surprised her. It was at
the end of their lesson when she had sung as usual
and he had listened to her with his usual pained face.
But before he went, he suddenly said it was time she
sang before an audience. She was so astonished, she
couldn't answer for a while, and when she could, it
was only to say "I didn't know." She meant she
didn't know he thought she was good enough for
that. He seemed to understand and it annoyed him.
He said "Why do you think I come here," and got up
to go downstairs. She followed him but he didn't
turn back and didn't speak to her again, he was so
irritated with her. And she longed for him to say

more, to tell her *why* he came, for once to hear from him that she had talent : but he left the house and turned down the street and she looked after him. He was tall, lean, and rather shabby, and walked like a person who is not in a hurry and has no particular destination. She didn't know where he went after he left her or how he spent his time; she guessed, however, that he didn't spend much of it at his home. When he had turned the corner she went back into the house. She was triumphant that day with joy. She even had visions of the marquee where the concerts took place and saw herself sitting on the stage, in the centre of a group of musicians. There would only be a thin and scattered audience — most people didn't bother to come till later when it was time for the important musician to start — nor would they be paying much attention, the way audiences don't pay much attention to the preliminaries before the big fight. But she would be there, singing, and not only for herself and her teacher. Yes, that was beautiful too, she loved it, but there had to be something more, she knew that; she had to give another dimension to her singing by performing before strangers. Now she realised she longed to do so. But she also knew it was not to be thought of. She was a housewife from a fine respectable middle-class family — people like her didn't sing in public. It would be an outrage, to her husband, to Phuphiji, to Manju's husband and Manju's in-laws. Even little Baba would be shocked, he wouldn't know what to think if he saw his granny singing before a lot of strangers.

That day she had another surprise. Her husband came home with a packet which he threw in her

direction, saying laconically "Take". She opened it
and, when she saw the contents, a lightning flash of
pleasure passed through her. It was a pair of ear-rings,
24-carat gold set with rubies and pearls. Her husband
watched her hooking them into her ears, pleased with
her and pleased with his purchase. He explained to her
how he had got them cheaply, as a bargain, from a
fellow contractor who was in difficulties and had been
forced to sell his wife's jewellery. Shakuntala locked
them away carefully in her steel safe in which she
kept all her other ornaments. Next day she took them
out again and wore them and looked at herself this
side and that. While she was doing this, Phuphiji came
in and, seeing the ear-rings, let out a cry. "Hai, hai!"
she cried, and came up and touched them as they
dangled from Shakuntala's ears. Shakuntala took them
off and locked them up again with the other things,
though not before Phuphiji's eyes had devoured them
in every detail. "He brought for you?" Phuphiji enquired and Shakuntala nodded briefly and turned the
key of the safe and fastened the bunch back to the
string at her waist. Suddenly Phuphiji was sitting on
the bed, weeping. She wept over the good fortune of
some and the ill fortune of others who had been
left widows at an early age and had no one to care for
them. When Shakuntala had nothing to say to comfort
her, she comforted herself and, wiping the corners of
her eyes with the end of her sari, said it was fate,
there was nothing to be done about it. It was the way
things were ordained in this particular life — though
next time, who knew, everything might come out
quite differently; wheels always came full circle and
those that were kings and queens now might, at the

next turn, find themselves nothing more than ants or some other form of lowly insect. This thought cheered her, and she went out and sat on the verandah and called to the servant-boy for a glass of hot tea.

Over the next few days, Shakuntala kept taking out her new ear-rings. She also took out some of her other pieces and admired them and put them on before the mirror. She loved gold and precious stones and fine workmanship; she also loved to see these things sparkling on herself and the effect they made against her skin and set off all her good points. She preened herself before the mirror and smiled like a girl. One afternoon, when she had spent some time in this pleasant way, she came out and found her teacher sitting on the blue sofa in the drawingroom. Phuphiji had as usual taken up her place near him. She was staring at him and he was yawning widely. They looked like two people who had been sitting there for a long time with nothing to say to each other. Shakuntala went out into the kitchen and quickly got some refreshments ready. Phuphiji followed her. "What's the use?" she said. "He won't eat, his stomach is not accustomed to these things." But that day he did eat, very quickly and ravenously like a man who has had nothing for some time. Shakuntala, watching him, saw that there was something wolf-like about him when he ate like that; she also noticed that he looked more haggard and unkempt than usual. And just before leaving, when he was already by the door, he asked her for an advance of salary. He asked quite casually and without embarrassment; it was she who was embarrassed. She went into the bedroom to take out her money. Phuphiji followed and whispered urgently "He

asked for money? Don't give him." Shakuntala ignored
her. She went out and gave it to him and he put it
in his pocket without counting and walked away without saying anything further.

Next morning, however, after she had finished
singing, he said that it was good she had given him
that money, it had come in very useful. She didn't
ask anything, out of delicacy, but he volunteered the
information that there was some "domestic upset".
He said this with a shrug and a laugh, not out of
bravado but really, obviously, because it didn't matter
to him. Then also she realised that his whole domestic
set-up — his dirty room, his quarrelsome wife — which
had so unpleasantly affected her, that too didn't
matter to him and her pity was misplaced. On the
contrary, today as she watched him walk away down
the street, in his shabby grey-white clothes and his
downtrodden slippers, she envied him. She thought
how he went where he liked and did what he liked.
Her own circumstances were so different. All that
day Phuphiji was after her, she nagged at her, she
kept asking how much money she had given him, why
had she given him, had her husband been told that
this money had been given? At last Shakuntala went
into her bedroom and bolted the door from inside.
It was a very hot day, and the room was close and
humid and mosquitoes buzzed inside with stinging
noises. Partly out of boredom, partly in the hope of
cheering herself up, she unlocked her jewellery again;
but now it failed to give her pleasure. It was just
things, metal.

Someone rattled at the door, she shouted "No, no!"
But it was Manju. She unbolted the door and opened

it just sufficiently to let Manju in; Phuphiji hovered behind but Shakuntala quickly shut her out. Manju saw her mother's jewellery spread out on the bed. She at once detected the new ear-rings and picked them up and asked where they had come from. "Put them on," Shakuntala invited her, and Manju lost no time in doing so. She looked in the mirror and liked herself very much in them. She went back to the bed and played with the other ornaments. One day they would all be hers but that day was still far off. She looked wistful and Shakuntala guessed what she was thinking and it made her want to pile everything into Manju's lap right now and say "Take it." And indeed when Manju, sighing a bit, put up her hand to take the ear-rings off again, Shakuntala suddenly said "You can keep them." Manju was astonished, she tried to protest, she said "Papa will be angry;" but her mother insisted. Then Manju returned to the mirror, she admired herself more than ever and a pleased smile of proprietorship lit up her somewhat glum features. Shakuntala stood behind her at the mirror. She too smiled with pleasure, though she could see that the ear-rings didn't suit Manju as well as they suited herself. This made her kiss her all the more tenderly. She was glad to see Manju happy with the gift.

For herself, nothing nowadays seemed to make her happy. Not even her early morning singing. Yet she was making good progress. It was one of those periods when she was beginning to master something that had up till then defeated her : now she saw that it lay

within her power, a little more effort and she would
be there and then she could begin to set her sights
on the next impossible step. But, in spite of this
triumph, she was dissatisfied and she knew her teacher
was too. Once or twice he had again broached the
subject of her singing in public; each time she had had
to put him off, by silence, by a sad smile. He knew
her reasons, of course, but did not sympathise with
them. Once he even told her, then what is the use?
And she knew he was right — what *was* the use — if
it was all to be locked up here in the house and no
one to hear, no one to care, no other heart to be
touched and respond. And all around her the birds
tumbled about in the bright air and sang out lustily,
pouring themselves out without stint. She fell into
despondency at herself, but her teacher was angry.
He said what did she expect, that he came here to
waste his time on training *housewives*? Then she began
to be afraid that he would stop coming and every
morning she got up and went on the roof with her
heart beating in fear; and how it leaped in relief when
he did come — cross usually, and sour, and displeased
with her, but he was there, he hadn't yet given her up.

He didn't come so often in the afternoons any
more, and when he did come, he stayed for a shorter
time. It seemed he was bored and restless there. Now
his glance of disdain fell not only on the refreshments
but on all the shiny furniture and the calendars and
the pictures on the wall. And most of all on Phuphiji.
Her presence, which he had before accepted with such
equanimity, now irritated him intensely. He made no
attempt to hide this, but Phuphiji did not care : she
kept right on sitting there, and when any comment

occurred to her she made it. His visit usually ended in his jumping up and hurrying away, muttering to himself. Once, when he had got outside the door, he said to Shakuntala "You should burn her, that's the only thing old women are good for, burning." Shakuntala's mouth corners twitched with amusement, but he was not in a joking mood. Next morning he asked her for another loan and she was glad to give it. He frequently asked her for money now. He ceased to make the excuse that it was an advance on salary, he just asked for the money and then pocketed it as if it were his right. He never counted it, the transaction was too trifling for him to bother that much about it.

It was not in the least trifling to Phuphiji. Although Shakuntala tried to keep these loans secret, it was not easy — indeed not possible — to keep anything that went on in the house secret from Phuphiji. She kept asking questions about the teacher's salary and whether he had taken any advance and, if so, how much; and when Shakuntala said she didn't remember, Phuphiji reproached her, she said that was not the way to deal with her husband's money. Once she caught them at it. She had hidden herself behind the water-butt in the courtyard and came pouncing out just as Shakuntala untied a bundle of notes and passed them to the teacher. Oh, asked Phuphiji, she was paying him his salary? That was strange, she said, it wasn't the first of the month, it wasn't anywhere near the first, it was somewhere about the middle of the month and surely that wasn't the time for paying anyone's salary? Before she could get any further, the teacher had taken out the money and flung it at her feet. Phuphiji jumped back a step or two as if it were some dangerous explosive. "Look at that," she cried, "see how he behaves!" But Shakuntala swooped down on the notes and picked them up and ran after him. He was already half-way down the street and didn't turn round. She had to implore him to stop. When he did, she thrust the money into his hand and he took it and stuffed it carelessly into his pocket and then continued his progress down the street.

Phuphiji would have dearly liked to complain to Shakuntala's husband, but she dared not. Indeed, she could not, for Shakuntala's husband never listened to her; if she wanted anything from him, she always had to approach him through Shakuntala. All she could do now was hover around him while he sat and ate his food. She shook out cushions that didn't need shaking, she waved away flies that weren't there, and talked to herself darkly in soliloquy. When she became too obtrusive, he turned to Shakuntala and asked "What's she say? What does the old woman want?" Then Phuphiji left off and went to sit outside, squatting on the floor with her knees hunched up and her head supported on her fist like a woman in mourning. Sometimes she used the supporting fist to strike her brow.

But she was more successful with Manju. She managed, by hints rather than by direct narration, to convey a sense of unease, even danger to Manju. She mentioned no figures but gave the impression that large sums of money were changing hands and that the teacher and all his family were being kept in luxury on money supplied by Shakuntala. "I hear they are buying a television set," Phuphiji whispered. "Can you

imagine people like that, who never had five rupees
to their name? A television set! Where do they get it
from?" And Manju drew back from Phuphiji's face
thrust close into hers, in shock and fright. Shakuntala
came in and found them like that. "What's the matter?"
she asked, looking from one to the other. "We're just
having a talk," Phuphiji said.

Another day Phuphiji hinted that it was not only
money that was going out of the house but other
things too.

"What?" Manju, who was not very quick, asked her.

"Very precious things," Phuphiji said.

Manju faltered : "Not — ?"

Phuphiji nodded and sighed.

"Her *jewellery*?" Manju asked, hand on heart.

Phuphiji stared into space.

"Oh God," Manju said. She caught up little Baba
and held him in a close embrace as if to protect him
against unscrupulous people out to rob him of his
inheritance. Baba began to cry. Manju cried with him,
and so did Phuphiji, two hard little tears dropping
from her as if squeezed from eyes of stone.

"It's true, she's in a strange mood," Manju said.
She told Phuphiji how her mother had given her the
new ear-rings : for no reason at all, had just waved her
hand and said casually "Take them". That was not
the way to give away jewellery, no not even to
your own daughter. It showed a person was strange.
And who knew, if she was in that kind of mood,
what she would do next — was perhaps already
doing — perhaps she was already telling other people
"Take them" in that same casual way, waving her
hand negligently over all that was most precious.

to a woman and a family. The thought struck horror into Phuphiji and Manju, and when Shakuntala came in, they both looked up at her as if she were someone remote from and dangerous to them.

Shakuntala hardly noticed them. Her thoughts were day and night elsewhere, and she longed only to be sitting on the roof practising her singing while her teacher listened to her. But nowadays he seemed to be bored with her. He tended to stay for shorter periods, he yawned and became restless and left her before she had finished. When he left her like that, she ceased to sing but continued to sit on the roof by herself; she breathed heavily as if in pain, and indeed her sense of unfulfilment was like pain and stayed with her for the rest of the day. The worst was when he did not turn up at all. This was happening more and more frequently. Days passed and she didn't see him and didn't sing; then he came again — she would step up on the roof in the morning, almost without hope, and there he would be. He had no explanation to offer for his absence, nor did she ask for one. She began straightaway to sing, grateful and happy. She was also grateful and happy when he asked her for money; it seemed such a small thing to do for him. Phuphiji noticed everything — his absences, her loans. She said nothing to Shakuntala but watched her. Manju came often and the two of them sat together and Phuphiji whispered into Manju's ear and Manju cried and looked with red, reproachful eyes at her mother.

One evening Manju and Phuphiji were both present while Shakuntala was serving her husband his meal. When he had finished and was dabbling his hand in the finger-bowl held for him by his wife, Phuphiji suddenly got up and, stepping close to Shakuntala, stood on tiptoe to look at her ears. She peered and squinted as if she couldn't see very well : she with eyes as sharp as little needles! "Are they new?" she asked.

"He gave them to me when Manju was born," Shakuntala replied quite calmly and even smiled a bit at the transparency of Phuphiji's tactics.

"Ah," said Phuphiji and paused. Her nose itched, she scratched it by pressing the palm of her hand against it and rubbing it round and round. When she had finished and emerged with her nose very red and tears in her eyes from this exertion, she said "But he gave you some new ones?"

"Yes," Shakuntala said.

"I haven't seen them," Phuphiji said. She turned to Manju : "Have you?"

Manju was silent. Shakuntala could feel that she was very tense, and so was Phuphiji. Both of them were anxious as to the outcome of this scene. But Shakuntala found herself to be completely indifferent.

Phuphiji turned to Shakuntala's husband : "Have you seen them?" she asked. "Where are they? Those new ear-rings you gave her?"

Shakuntala knew that Phuphiji and Manju were both waiting for her to speak so that they could deny what she was going to say. But she said nothing and only handed the towel to her husband to dry his hands. She didn't want Manju to have to say or do anything that would make her feel very bad afterwards.

"Why don't you ask her?" Phuphiji said. "Go on, ask her : where are those new ear-rings I gave you? Ask. Let's hear what she has to say."

For one second her husband looked at Shakuntala; his eyes were like those of an old bear emerging from his winter sleep. But the next moment he had flung down the towel and stamped on it in rage. He shouted at Phuphiji and abused her. He said he didn't come home to be pestered and needled by a pack of women, that's not what he expected after his hard day's work. He also shouted at Manju and asked her why sit on his back, let her go home and sit on her husband's back, what else had she been married off for at enormous expense? Manju burst into tears, but that was nothing new and no one tried to comfort her, not even Phuphiji who busied herself with clearing away the dirty dishes, patient and resigned in defeat.

That night passed slowly for Shakuntala. She lay beside her husband and was full of restless thoughts. But when morning came and her teacher again failed to show up, then she did not hesitate any longer. She went straight to his house. She walked through his courtyard where they were hammering pieces of plywood together, up the stairs, past the music school, and up to his door. It had a big padlock on it. She was put out, but only for a moment. She went down to the music school. Several thin men in poor clothes sat on the floor testing out drums and tuning stringed instruments; they looked at her curiously, and even more curiously when she asked for him. They shrugged at each other and laughed. "God knows," they said. "Ever since she went, he's here and there." "Who went?" Shakuntala asked. They looked at her again and wondered. "His wife," one of them said at last. Shakuntala was silent and so were they. She didn't know what else to ask. She turned and went down the stairs. One of them followed and looked down at her from the landing. As if in afterthought he called : "He sits around in the restaurants!" She walked through the courtyard where they stopped hammering and also looked after her with curiosity.

Shakuntala had lived in the town all her life, but she was only familiar with certain restricted areas of it. There were others that she knew of, had seen and of necessity passed through on her way to somewhere else, but which remained mysterious and out of bounds to her. One of these was the street where the singing and dancing girls lived, and another was the street where the restaurants were. The two were connected, and to get to the restaurants Shakuntala had first to pass through the other street. This was lined with shops selling coloured brassieres, scents, and filigree necklaces, and on top of the shops were balconies on which the girls sat. Downstairs stood little clusters of men with betel-stained mouths; they looked at Shakuntala and some of them made sweet sounds as she passed. Here and there from upstairs came the sound of ankle-bells and a few bars tapped out for practice on a drum. The street of the restaurants was much quieter. No sounds came out from behind the closed doors of the restaurants. They were called *Bombay House, Shalimar, Monna Lisa, Taj Mahal*. Shakuntala hesitated only before the first one and even then only for a moment before pushing open the door. They were mostly alike from inside with a lot of peeling plaster-of-paris decorations and a smell of fried food, tobacco, and perfumed oil. The clientele was alike too. There was no woman among them, and Shakuntala's presence attracted attention. There was some laughter and, despite her age, also the sweet sounds she had heard from the men in the streets.

She found him in the third one she entered (*Bombay House*). He was one of a group lounging against the wall on a red leather bench behind a table cluttered with plates and glasses. He was drumming one hand rhythmically on the table and swaying and dipping his head in time to a tune playing inside it. When Shakuntala stepped up to the table, the other men sitting with him were astonished; their jaws stopped chewing betel and dropped open. Only he went on swaying and drumming to the tune in his mind. He let her stand there for a while, then he said to the others "She's my pupil. I teach her singing." He added "She's a housewife," and sniggered. No one else said anything nor moved. She noticed that his eyes were heavy and with a far-away blissful look in them.

He got up and, tossing some money on the table, left the restaurant. She followed him, back the same way she had come past the restaurants and through the street of the singing and dancing girls. He walked in front all the time. He was still singing the same tune to himself and was still at the introductory stage, letting the raga develop slowly and spaciously. His hand made accompanying gestures in the air. He also waved this hand at people who greeted him on the way and sometimes to the girls when they called down to him from the balconies. He seemed to be a well-known figure. Walking behind him, Shakuntala remembered the many times she had stood in the doorway of her house watching him as he walked, slowly and casually like someone with all time at his disposal, away from her down the street; only now she did not have to turn back into her house, no she was following him and going where he was going. The tune he was singing began in her mind too and she smiled to it and let it unfold itself in all its glory.

He led the way back to his house and they walked up the stairs, and first the men in the courtyard and then the men in the music school looked after them. He unfastened the big padlock on his door. Inside everything was as before when she had visited him in his sickness except that the sewing-machine was gone and the air was denser because no one had opened the window for a long time. His bedding, consisting of a mat and tumbled sheet, was as he must have left it in the morning. He wasted no time but at once came close to her and fumbled at her clothes and at his own. He was about the same age as her husband but lean, hard, and eager; as he came on top of her, she saw his drugged eyes so full of bliss and he was still smiling at the tune he was playing to himself. And this tune continued to play in her too. He entered her at the moment when, the structure of the raga having been expounded, the combination of notes was being played up and down, backwards and forwards, very fast. There was no going back from here, she knew. But who would want to go back, who would exchange this blessed state for any other?

*   *   *

L

Suffering Women

Anjana had never been a top film star, but she had done well enough to be able to retire comfortably. Now she lived in a very nice flat with lofty ceilings in one of the old Bombay houses and her daughter Kiku went to college and even spoke of going to America for higher studies. Anjana didn't intend to send her to America, but she liked to hear her talk about it. Many of Kiku's friends also intended to go to America for higher studies.

Anjana was proud of the friends Kiku had. They all came from very good backgrounds; their parents were professional or business people, and some of them belonged to Bombay's smart social set. Anjana was amazed at the freedom their children were allowed. Boys and girls who not only were not related but even came from different castes and communities went out together wherever they liked and with the full consent of their parents. Kiku had a boy friend too — Rahul — and it was so sweet to see them go out together, dancing or parties or a day on the beach; both of them were quite tall and very slim and wore the latest gay clothes.

When Kiku had first proposed going out with Rahul, Anjana had forbidden her to do so. She had shouted at Kiku and told her how she would be getting a bad name. Kiku had shouted back and they had had one of their scenes. On this occasion, as on most others, Kiku had won. Anjana had begun to be persuaded that times had changed and that everyone went out with boy friends now. Many impressive examples were cited (Shirin Mehta of the oil Mehtas, Leila Handa who had gone to school in Switzerland); finally Rahul himself was brought to the flat and made such a superb impression that the last shreds of the mother's fears could not but be blown away. Anjana saw at once that both her daughter and her daughter's reputation were absolutely safe with Rahul. A more well-bred, careful, *harmless* boy did not exist.

Long after Anjana had resigned herself to Rahul and had indeed learned to rejoice in him, Thakur Sahib was still dissatisfied. Thakur Sahib was Anjana's lover. They had been together for many years. Thakur Sahib was married and had several daughters of his own. Although he was a film producer and moved among easy-living people, he kept his daughters very strictly — perhaps more strictly than a man less conversant with what went on in the world might have done. He didn't care for the freedom Kiku was allowed, and he especially didn't care for her to go out with Rahul. Anjana explained about the modern world and changing society, just as Kiku had explained to her, but Thakur Sahib pushed out his lips in a sceptical way. Anjana became annoyed with him. She said he was old and stubborn and his attitude made him ridiculous in the eyes of intelligent people. His only reply was to push out his lips further.

He was lying on Anjana's bed in her bedroom on her pink velvet bedspread. She would have liked to fold it back to prevent it from getting spoiled, but she didn't care to disturb him once he had made himself comfortable. And he was very comfortable : his paunch, with his hands folded on top of it, rose mightily above the bed and breathed up and down.

Anjana said "There is no harm at all. They're just two children — a little boy and girl playing together."

Thakur Sahib's lids had sunk like rolling shutters to cover his eyes, leaving only a small knowing glint shining out at her from underneath. He said, in a calm, comfortable voice, that there was only one game little boys and girls played together. Anjana got very angry and shouted at him for his bad thoughts. But he was unrepentant and continued to lie there, unmoving, so that she knew it was no use shouting any further. He was one of the few people she had had in her life who would not participate in a scene. When she tried to start one with him, he always shrugged her off — with an indifference which, in spite of the fury it inspired in her, she could not help admiring : for its strength, its manliness.

She sank down by the side of the bed and, taking his feet between her hands, began to massage them. They were surprisingly small and delicate feet. She loved them. She pressed and squeezed them and pulled each toe till it ticked and he cried out in ecstasy. Each cry was an inspiration to her. She knew that never in his life had he had anyone who knew how to massage the way she did. His wife had no skill at all. Now Anjana massaged him even when she went to visit him in his own house (and she was an unquestioned visitor there now; after initial difficulties, everything had settled down very nicely). His wife watched and didn't mind. She had accepted the fact that it was not in her power to give him pleasure and had become indifferent to seeing him get it from others. Sometimes, watching, she shrugged and smiled in a superior

way, as one who had long since left all such things
behind her.

"Last night they went dancing," Anjana said, while
he lay there made helpless and soft. "All the young
people go." She gave his ankles a squeeze so delicate,
so refined that any man's soul would have been
charmed out of his body. "I wish you could have
seen them. He came to fetch her in his father's car.
He was wearing trousers — tight, tight!" She showed
how tight and laughed. "Such a slim boy. Not like
some people;" she laughed again and hit her fist against
Thakur Sahib's hips which shook like a woman's. But
then she made a kissing sound into the air to show
how much all the same she loved him. More than all
the slim boys in the world! "And Kiku had her new
orange silk kameez with pearl embroidery all down
here. She has such taste, that child, like a princess. And
you should hear her talking with the tailor. Each little
stitch has to be just right, or she makes him open it all
up again. Oh she's strict with them! Of course they
charge — everybody charges — the material, if I told
you what it cost. But I'm there for the bill, why
worry." She had worked her way up from his feet to
his knees now : he lay and enjoyed; she could say
anything she liked. She knew he did not approve of
Kiku's extravagant taste or of the very modern way
she dressed either. His own girls' wardrobe was much
more modest in both price and style. Of course their
looks too were not like Kiku's.

"He brought flowers for her and chocolate marzipan
from Bombelli's," she said. "He's such a sweet boy.
And what a *gentleman*. But she treats him — well,
you know how she is with everybody. She's the queen

and the rest of the world has to be her slave. She didn't even say thank you for the flowers and chocolates — didn't look at them, as if they were nothing. But I know she was pleased, don't I know her. And she was pleased to be fetched in a car and she could hardly *wait* to get to that place they go for dancing, though she pretended it wasn't anything and she would just as soon stay at home. She even said to him : 'Why don't we stay home and play cards with Mamma.' Yes, in her new kameez — I can just see her staying at home to play cards with me!" She had been merry up till then, but on that she sighed and became philosophical : "Let the old stay at home, when you're young, that's the time. It won't come back again. Do you like it?" she whispered to him, her fingers sinking deep into his thighs. "Am I doing it well?" He put out his hand and — fond, familiar, and grateful — he patted her.

"Why grudge their happiness," she said. "What's left for us? Now at this age."

Then he said something which a man of means and standing like Thakur Sahib will only say to his most intimate friend in their most intimate moments. For decency's sake, she suppressed a smile, though it would hardly be suppressed; and to punish him, she touched him in that place between his thighs her ministrations had now reached. In spite of what she had said, she felt at that moment that she and Thakur Sahib were not old at all but, on the contrary, quite young and mischievous.

Anjana's best friend was a lady called Sultana. Anjana had long since retired as a film actress, but

Sultana still kept going. Of course she could no longer play the heroine's part, but was mostly cast in a subsidiary elderly role such as mother-in-law. She had made a speciality of that kind of part so that when she appeared on the screen everyone knew what to expect. She was a lot in demand and never dared to turn a part down for fear of not being asked again. As a result she was much busier than at her age she ought to have been and got quite worn out by the constant long shooting schedules and travelling to and fro.

"Why don't you give it up?" Anjana asked her one day when Sultana came to her looking even more tired than usual. She had come straight from the set and now lay reclining with her shoes off in Anjana's drawingroom. They were having tea and rather a lot to eat with the tea : stuffed pancakes, Bengali milk puffs swimming in cream, cashew-nuts spiced with chili powder, egg sandwiches, and cakes covered with pink icing. Anjana kept pushing the dishes towards Sultana but Sultana only nibbled a bit here and there without appetite, while it was Anjana herself who enjoyed everything as food should be enjoyed.

Anjana advised her friend : "You ought to retire and just lead a nice fat lazy life like I do." She smiled in a fat lazy way.

Sultana didn't smile. Her mouth corners turned down further and she shrugged : "Yes, and what about this?" she asked with some bitterness, rubbing two fingers together to suggest money.

Anjana spoke a drawn-out "Oh" and made a deprecatory gesture with her hand : "A rich woman like you."

"Ha," laughed Sultana with more bitterness.

Anjana knew very well that Sultana, in spite of her considerable earnings in the past and present, was not rich at all. She could have been, but she had one terrible extravagance : she was always falling in love with young men. Some of these young men were aspiring film actors, others liked to lead a life devoted to art and culture. In either case, they were rather demanding and had expensive tastes. So Sultana had to go on working.

"How is Sayyid?"

"He is redecorating the apartment," Sultana replied without pleasure. Sayyid was the latest young man, an interior decorator.

"What, again!" cried Anjana.

"He says he needs practice."

There was an unhappy silence. Anjana imagined how Sultana came home exhausted from the set to find her apartment full of paint and workmen and Sayyid running around irritably giving orders. There would be nowhere for her to sit and be comfortable, the way she was comfortable here with Anjana. If she tried to stretch out on a sofa in a corner, Sayyid would tell her "Not there please, darling," and he would order the workmen to push the sofa away before she had quite had time to get up again. And afterwards, when it was all done, what prospect of comfort did she have even then? Sayyid went in for very modern furniture; he also liked very modern pictures on the wall, mostly painted by his friends.

Anjana got up and tucked a huge satin cushion behind the other's back. She ran her fingers loving-ly over Sultana's face : how tired she looked, her poor friend. "Rest now," she murmured. "Be quite comfortable." Sultana gratefully shut her eyes and murmured back "It's so nice here."

It *was* nice. Kiku was always trying to get her mother to have the room redone in a modern style, but Anjana liked it the way it was. She had done up everything in royal blue velvet — she loved velvet best of all, it was almost alive it was so soft and sensuous — and where there wasn't velvet there was satin, and a carpet with flowers and vines and tigers and parrots woven into it; the furniture was heavy and intricately carved the way she had glimpsed it in rich people's houses when she was young; there were many ornaments such as vases with Japanese ladies on them, and china dogs, and dolls in quaint costumes. On the wall hung Anjana's favourite picture : a pale lady draped in diaphonous white sitting on a rock and looking out over the sea with wild, sad eyes, her arms clasped about her knees, her long hair blowing in the wind.

While Sultana rested, Anjana told her about Kiku and Rahul. But Sultana did not even make a pretence of being interested; she lay with her eyes shut and only opened them to look at her nails and blow a speck of dust off them. It was always like that with her. She wasn't interested in Kiku, and whenever Anjana spoke about her, she became bored. Of course this was because she had never had a child of her own and did not have a heart big enough to rejoice in the happiness of others.

Anjana gave a great sigh both of resignation and contentment : "What other pleasure is there left to us except what we get from out children?"

Sultana yawned. She didn't open her mouth to

do so, but instead she swallowed the yawn and made
a pained face as if it were something unpleasant she
had swallowed.

"It's a pity," Anjana said, "you don't have some
young people about you. It would help you to keep
yourself young and not feel so tired all the time."

Of course as soon as she had said this, Anjana
realised her mistake. Sultana threw her a quick ironic
look. She had always been famous for her eyes which
were not full, dark, and passionate like Anjana's, but
disturbingly light-coloured (Sultana claimed Persian
ancestry) and flecked with cold, fierce lights like those
of a tigress.

Anjana's anger grew at having these famous eyes
used on her. She cried "The only way to know and
love the young is as a mother!"

Sultana also became angry but, as usual when this
happened, she did not shout but smiled (showing her
small, slightly pointed teeth which were still as white
as in her youth and almost as perfect) and sent lights
to flicker from her eyes.

"Look at you," said Anjana, holding out her hand
and waving it to and fro to indicate her friend's
reclining figure. "So tired you can hardly breathe and
now you have to go home and play with your Sayyid.
I *pity* you," she added, twisting her lips in a contemptuous rather than pitying way.

"Thank you," said Sultana, "but I'd rather have
someone to laugh and play than a fat old man snoring
on my bed."

Anjana could not, on the spur of the moment,
think of anything insulting enough to reply, so she
said in a very mean voice and with a mean expression

on her face : "If you knew how people talked about you."

"Let them talk," said Sultana. She sat up on the sofa and began to grope for her shoes with her feet.

"I feel ashamed when I hear the things that are said about you. I want to get angry with people, to say she is my friend, it's not true, but how can I when it *is* true. Lie down, what are you sitting up for."

Sultana wriggled her feet into her shoes, one at a time, wearily.

"Now I suppose you want to run away. A little bit of truth and you run. Go on, lie *down*." She leaned forward and gave the other a push that sent her sprawling back on the sofa. Sultana lay where she fell and made no further attempt to move.

Anjana said "Who else will tell you if I don't? Who else have you got in this world to care for you the way I care? Ridiculous — working like a — like a — and for what? So that you can keep some young — some little — no all right, I'll be quiet!" she cried as Sultana opened her dangerous eyes. "I'll say nothing!" She poured more tea into Sultana's cup and said in a fury "Drink this."

"I don't want," Sultana said with closed eyes.

"*Drink* it!"

Sultana turned her face away. Her eyes remained closed. Anjana knew she would not take the tea. She stood holding it and looking down into Sultana's face, exasperated by its expression of obstinacy and both exasperated and pained by the exhaustion so clearly written there.

"Don't drink," Anjana said, setting the cup down

with a clatter and bang. "Don't eat, don't drink. Kill yourself. That's the best way."

Anjana and Sultana had known each other for more than thirty years. During that time their relationship had had many ups and downs. Years had passed during which they had not been on speaking terms. Other years they had been like sisters. In their youth, in the heyday of their careers, they had been professional rivals. They had both played heroines in the same kind of second-grade films; both had been very popular among taxi-drivers, wrestlers, and small boys queueing up for the four-anna seats on Saturday mornings. Sultana, with her tigress eyes and lithe figure, had played bold, manly parts and had been cheered out of thousands of throats as she galloped over the Khyber Pass, clutching in her arms the infant king whom she had rescued in the nick of time from his black-bearded murderers. Anjana, on the other hand, all soft bosom and melting eyes, had been made love to in trellissed bowers and danced ankle-deep in meadows of white primroses. Off-screen, they were both equally romantic and had been remarkable for the number and intensity of their love affairs. It was here, and not in their professional lives, that their rivalry had for a time turned into bitter enmity.

The cause had been Kiku's father. They had both been in love with him, and he had inclined first to one and then to the other. Finally, when she became pregnant, Anjana had got him to marry her. Sultana's rage and anguish had known no bounds, although it became clear quite soon that it was Anjana who had had the worst of it. Kiku's father had never forgiven her for their marriage. It was not only that he was a Muslim and she a Hindu, but also that he came from an old Lucknow family claiming descent from courtiers, while Anjana's mother and grandmother (like Sultana's) had been dancing-girls. He could not forget his fall, and she too had become deeply imbued with feelings of guilt. She did all she could to make it up to him, keeping him in the luxury that he loved and pampering him in all his desires and manifold tastes. Nothing did any good. Sick with self-disgust, he became more slothful, more bitter, drank all night and slept all day, wrote poetry squashy with too many nightingales and roses and laments for the transience of all worldly delights : till finally he was found dead from taking a combination of drink and drugs which he may or may not have known to be fatal in effect. Anjana and Sultana had a reconciliation scene over his bier worthy of one of their own films; but their high-flown language, the torn hair and clothes, the wailing and the breast-beating were real. Passion and grief had torn their hearts in two, and when they mended again they were found to have grown together in a rough jagged way and could not be parted again.

Kiku was not ready when Rahul came to fetch her, so Anjana made him comfortable in the drawingroom and sat by him to keep him company. But she did not feel easy. It may have been his too good, too deferential manners; and the thought of his aristocratic parents in their fashionable home and what they would think if they saw him sitting there talking to her; and what if she said something wrong, which

might undermine his opinion not only of her but of
Kiku too on her account? It was a relief to her when
Kiku was ready at last and came into the drawingroom, clicking on high heels, a flower cunningly
entwined in her hair. She did not apologise for having
kept him waiting, but on the contrary made it seem
as if he were keeping her : "Well come on! What are
you waiting for? New Year?"

Anjana watched them leave from her bedroom
window. His car was parked on the pavement several
storeys below her. She watched him open the car
door for her, watched Kiku glide gracefully in. They
drove off. Anjana looked up to the sky and prayed :
God, bless them. From the sky her eyes reluctantly
came down again to the building opposite. Once she
had had a wonderful view of the sea from her bedroom
window, but some five years ago a building as tall as
her own had been built on the site opposite. It was
a private nursing-home. Some of the patients were
permanent inmates and had probably been placed there
by rich relatives unwilling to keep them at home. The
same woman had stood at the window facing Anjana's
ever since the place had opened. Hour after hour she
looked out over the iron bars which reached half-way
up the window. At first Anjana had tried to make
friendly overtures to her but when she got no response
at all, when the woman had simply gone on staring
in the same blank way, Anjana had realised that she
was not right in her mind.

Anjana drew the curtains, she turned on the lamps.
The curtains were of pink velvet, the lampshades pink
satin. She should have felt cosy and safe, but she felt
neither. She knew too well what terrible things can

happen. Kiku didn't know anything about that. She thought that if you had money and lived in a comfortable home nothing could touch you. Again Anjana raised her eyes in prayer, begging blessing and protection for her child. If only she could have been sure that there was someone to hear her! But all she saw was her white ceiling with a basket of roses moulded on it in plaster-of-paris. Sighing with pain, she went to the telephone and rang up Thakur Sahib. She needed him so much.

Thakur Sahib was not as young as he had been, and he got very tired running around all day dealing with financiers, film stars, and distributors. So it was not a small request, Anjana knew, to get him out again in the evening when he had settled down comfortably at home and had eaten his meal and was ready to go to sleep. All the same, he came at her call, and she was so grateful that she could not do enough for him. She made herself be gay and lively, talked a lot, and ran to and fro plying him with drinks and refreshments. He sat in the most comfortable chair in the room, propped up from every side by her satin cushions; behind him on the wall hung her favourite picture of the lady in white gazing over the sea. Anjana sat on the carpet at Thakur Sahib's feet and leaned her head against his knee; from time to time she took a sip from his glass, making a face at the taste of the whisky.

"Where's Kiku?" he asked.

"She's gone out." But she changed the subject quickly; she didn't want to have an argument with him today on the subject of Kiku. Instead she began talking to him about Sultana, telling him about her friend's money worries and the hard life she led.

Thakur Sahib said "Whose fault is that." He wasn't very sympathetic towards Sultana. As a matter of fact, he wasn't sympathetic towards any actress. He had to have a lot to do with them and of course made his money through them, but he didn't like them or approve of the way they lived.

"Poor thing," said Anjana, "she's looking so tired and old."

Thakur Sahib shrugged and took a drink from his glass. Then he said "That one came to see me today."

"Who?"

"What's her name — Tara Bai."

"Tara Bai!"

"I didn't recognise her. She looks like an old beggar-woman. The servants nearly drove her away."

"What did she want?"

"What do they always want."

"Money?"

"What else."

Anjana turned her face from him so that he would not see the expression on it. Tara Bai had been a very famous actress, a bigger star than either Sultana or Anjana. But she had had a troubled life, like so many others.

"Where is she living?" Anjana asked. Thakur Sahib didn't know and didn't care. Unable to stop herself, Anjana went on asking questions in a frightened, frenzied way : "What about her son? She had a son, from that musician she was with. Where is he? Why isn't he looking after his mother?"

"I gave her fifty rupees and didn't ask any questions.

I was glad to get rid of her." He noticed the look on Anjana's face : "What's the matter with you? Why should you care about these people?"

Anjana kept quiet. She didn't want to remind him that she too had been one of them. It was all different now — she had saved money and bought shares and lived respectably on the interest. Her daughter went to college. Why should she be afraid? She got up and refilled his glass, then perched on his knees and held the glass to his lips to make him drink. She pressed herself so closely against him that he could feel her heart beating through her ample warm flesh.

The telephone rang. Anjana went out to answer it. It was one of Thakur Sahib's daughters. After apologising for disturbing auntie (as she called Anjana), she asked to have a message delivered to her father. Anjana went to tell him : it was some business matter, a meeting to be arranged in the morning. At once the expression on his face changed and he became the busy film producer. He began to give her instructions what to reply on the telephone, but midway changed his mind and got up to answer himself. Anjana followed and listened to him talking to his daughter. She pointed to herself to indicate that she too would like to talk. He nodded, but at the end of his conversation he put down the receiver and returned to the room, engrossed in his thoughts.

"I wanted to talk," she said, following him.

"What?"

"I wanted to talk to her about her exam. Poor child, she was so worried. I wanted to ask her how she got on. And then you put it down. How does it look?"

"It doesn't matter."

M

"To you no, but what will the child think? She will say to herself, 'Just see, auntie doesn't care about me, she doesn't even ask.' "

"No one will think."

He spoke with curt authority, but she continued to brood. She thought of his family, his wife and daughters, and how wrong it was of her to call him away from them like this in the evening. She knew herself to be guilty. But her need of him was so great. She could not live without Thakur Sahib. If they parted, her life would be a dark tunnel, she would grope here and there and be lost and afraid. But what right, she asked herself, had she compared with *their* right? If they hated and cursed her, it would only be what she deserved. Suddenly she threw back her head and, flinging her hands before her face, rocked herself to and fro.

Thakur Sahib started forward in his chair and shouted "What is it? What is it?"

"You put it down on purpose! You don't want me to talk to her!"

"Madwoman!"

"You think I'm like Tara Bai, that I've led a bad life. And you're right : I *have* led a bad life. Very bad. Oh God!" She sobbed.

Thakur Sahib was angry. He tried to force her to uncover her face and look at him; but she wouldn't, and the angrier he grew, the more she said he was right to be angry with her. She said what she really deserved was for him to go away, go back to his family, leave her for ever. But when, cursing her obstinacy, he turned from her for a moment, she leaped up and, throwing herself on the floor, clasped

her arms around his knees and declared that if he
went, if he left her, she would kill herself. She even
described how she would kill herself, committing
suttee for his departure in the best tradition by
pouring kerosene over her clothes and setting herself
on fire.

She let go of his legs and stretched herself flat on
the floor. "Yes leave me," she said. "Let me lie here
and die." And indeed, she lay quite still on the floor,
as one dead already.

"Enough now," Thakur Sahib said quite calmly and
sat down in his armchair again. He drank what was
left of his whisky. Anjana sat up. She dried her eyes
with the end of her sari and scrambled up from the
floor, groaning as she did so for her knee was somewhat stiff and hurt her. She got back into her former
position on his lap, her arms entwined about his neck.
Over his shoulder she could see her picture of the
lady sitting on a rock and looking with suffering eyes
out over the sea. It was not hard to guess why she was
suffering. There was only one thing could fill a
woman's eyes with such expression, or indeed make
her hair fly with such wild abandon in the wind.
Anjana laid her lips on Thakur Sahib's cheek and
left them there. He had a strong growth and should
by rights have shaved twice a day, but she loved the
tough bristles poking her skin. She laid one hand on
the back of his head to bring him closer to her face.
She didn't like the taste of whisky, but she loved the
smell of it after he had drunk it.

When Sultana did not come to see her for more
than a week, Anjana became worried about her and

went to visit her. Sultana lived right on top of a very new tall white apartment building from where she had a wonderful view of the sea and other tall white apartment buildings. The apartment was very expensive, and the constant redecorating to which Sayyid subjected it also cost a great deal. On this visit Anjana found everything quite different from the last time she had been there. Sayyid had now entered a very austere stage : the walls were painted stark white, and what little furniture he had allowed himself was made of metal in sharp geometrical shapes.

Sultana was sitting on a comfortless, wrought-iron sofa, smoking a cigarette. She was wearing slacks in a leopard skin design and a shirt. Sultana was not fat, but she had the hips and bosom of an Indian woman and these burgeoned within the tight confines of her unaccustomed Western clothes. She looked up briefly when Anjana came in and went on smoking. Anjana knew at once that something had happened and that Sultana was in a very gloomy mood.

Anjana asked "Where's Sayyid?"

"God knows." Sultana shrugged bitterly.

So that was it : of course Anjana had easily guessed. Sultana had great shadows under her eyes and looked as if she had not slept for several nights. Anjana imagined her lying in bed, staring into the dark. Sultana hardly ever wept. Instead her tigress eyes became dry and hard, and one could imagine them gleaming in the dark like green stones.

"When did he go?" Anjana said.

"Four days ago." Sultana took a deep drag from her cigarette.

Anjana sighed; it was by no means a new situation.

Not only Sayyid but earlier young men too had tended to disappear from time to time and then Sultana sat at home and smoked and waited and suffered.

"He'll come back," Anjana said.

"Of course. When he's tired."

"Some girl?"

"Or boy." Sultana shrugged again.

Anjana's heart hurt for her so much she had to lay her hand on it and hold it. She knew what it was to have to wait for someone, pace the house and wonder what he was doing and with whom. Kiku's father used to disappear in the same way, before he had become too sunk in sloth and drink to want to move. And, with him too, one could never be sure in what company he had spent his time, whether it was some young girl or boy that had engaged his fancy.

Anjana asked "Did you have a quarrel?"

"We always have quarrels."

"No but anything special?"

"Everything is special. If I do my hair in a way he doesn't like, it's special. If I don't smile enough at his friends, that's special too. I must run here and there to serve them, otherwise I'm showing him disrespect. *I* show *him* disrespect! Can you imagine! That boy, half my age! Look!" She pushed up her sleeve; there was a scratch on her arm — nothing very bad, but Anjana cried out. "That was for showing him disrespect. To teach me a lesson. But don't worry, he got plenty in return." She laughed horribly. "Wherever he's gone, he's taken a few marks with him to show."

Anjana shook her head. God knew, she had gone through enough such scenes herself, but that had been long ago, when she was young and full of strength and spirit. "At your age," she told Sultana.

"I know! When all I want is peace and quiet! You know how I feel when I come home from shooting. But no, every night he's got some programme. And if I say I'm tired, then what scenes! Then how I'm spoiling, ruining his life! The names he calls me. Of course his favourite is old hag. It's all his own fault he says for getting himself entangled with an old hag."

"No," Anjana said, "it's not his fault. It's yours." She shifted uncomfortably on the little wrought-iron chair and it increased her temper. "How can you live like this? Not even a place to sit! No wonder you're going mad. I would go mad. Anyone would. And don't smoke so much," she added, for Sultana, having just ground out one half-smoked cigarette in the over-flowing ashtray, had at once lit another.

"There's no taste in them," Sultana said, filling herself up with smoke and blowing it out again in disgust through her nostrils.

It was Sayyid who had made her take to cigarettes. Before that she had smoked a hookah. She had had a very elaborate one with an enamelled base and a tube so long that it coiled and twisted into many rings. Sultana had reclined in her wide silk trousers on a silk-covered mattress, sucking at the silver mouthpiece while the hookah made soft soothing bubbling noises. In those days her room had always been thick and fragrant with a mixed smell of incense and tobacco. Now it didn't smell of anything.

"Listen," Anjana said, leaning urgently towards her friend. "You come home with me. Lock up this place, rent it out, do anything you like. But come with me. Now — at once! Where's Ayah?

Let her pack your things."

Sultana's eyes glittered with pleasure : "What a shock he'll have when he comes home and finds me gone! Oh I would like to see his face! Just to see his face!"

"Never mind about him. Where are your keys? Give them to me."

She held out her hand. Sultana lifted her shirt and fumbled for her keys which — in spite of her Western clothes — she kept on a string round her waist. She dropped them into Anjana's palm. But as soon as Anjana's fingers closed on them, she said "No, give them back."

"I won't. I'll take out your jewels and a few clothes and then we're going. Ayah can bring the rest to-morrow."

"I'll come tomorrow. I'll pack everything myself, that will be much better. Ayah doesn't know anything, she's so clumsy and stupid."

"We're going *now*."

Anjana held on tight to the keys. Sultana kept sitting and looking up at her with eyes which, in spite of their dry hard glitter, were almost appealing.

"Supposing he comes today — "

"So let him come. Very good."

"Yes but I want to see his face! When I tell him it's finished, I'm renting out the apartment, there's no place for you here any more. For you *or* your friends. How will he look then? What will he do?" Sultana ground her teeth : "I know what he'll do," she said with vicious pleasure. "He'll *cry*. He always cries when I'm really angry with him. Big tears." She showed with her fingers how the tears coursed down his cheeks. "Well this time I'll let him cry. I'll stand there and watch him." She folded her arms in satisfaction and fixed her eyes in space as if she actually saw him standing there crying. Anjana didn't say anything but she had her hands on hips and one foot tapped up and down and there was a cynical expression on her face.

"He'll have a surprise," Sultana said. "He thinks it will be like always — that I'll take him in my arms, lay his head in my lap and beg him, don't cry. When I say that he always cries more. He presses his face into my thighs and sobs and sobs. And I stroke his head." She stroked the air, with great tenderness.

Anjana opened the hand in which she had been clutching the keys and flung them towards Sultana. Sultana picked them up and fastened them back to the string at her waist. She laughed. She said "Well what can I do? He's so young, so lovely. Do you know he doesn't have one single hair on his chest? Smooth, smooth, like satin. Velvet," she said in a voice like velvet.

At home Kiku was busy with the tailor. She was wearing another new outfit — in rose silk — but something had displeased her about the fit of the trousers. The tailor had been summoned and now he crouched on the floor sewing at her ankles while she looked down at him severely. She was ready to go out, ready to the last exquisite detail, with brand-new varnish on each finger and toe-nail. Her hair was swept up and garnished with a rose.

"Is Rahul coming to fetch you?" Anjana asked.

"I suppose so." She stifled a yawn, then frowned

down at the tailor who responded by crouching lower and plying his needle with redoubled energy. Appeased, she looked up again and at her mother. Anjana sat enjoying a little snack she had ordered for herself. Now Kiku frowned at her : "Mamma, of course if you eat so much you must expect to get fat."

"But I'm fat already."

Kiku gave her a little lecture. She told her that even in middle age women had to keep themselves trim and slim and up to the mark. She gave her mother a few hints how to achieve this end, dwelling mainly on diet and exercise. Anjana respectfully listened. She was proud of Kiku's expertise and the forceful way in which she expounded it. Although so young, Kiku already knew so much and on so many interesting subjects.

Rahul arrived exactly on time. Anjana hastily sat up from her reclining position and fumbled at her dishevelled hair. He asked her permission to sit down and this flustered her, and in any case she was prevented from replying by having hair-pins in her mouth.

As always with Rahul, Anjana felt compelled to make conversation. She asked after his studies, his friends, his exams. He answered patiently; he was quite at his ease and sat with one leg crossed over the other. Anjana admired his calm, his confidence. It was obvious that here was a boy born to a good position in life which would be his without struggle or effort. He knew it himself, and consequently there was a smile of good-nature always hovering on his lips. Clearly he would never give trouble to any woman — would not fight with her or run off, worrying her

to death where he was gone and who he was with. One
could always be sure of him. A golden boy! Anjana
smiled and shook her head to herself : she admired
him so much. Yet at the same time as she looked at
him with this wistful admiration, there was some other
expression in her eyes as she — instinctively, almost
unconsciously — weighed him up to herself. Yes, it
was true, he wouldn't give trouble to a woman — but
was he the type to give her much pleasure either?
And her lips curled a little bit differently from a
smile of approval as her eyes measured him up and
down quite frankly now, so that he noticed and was
surprised and shifted a little bit on his chair. He had
never been looked at like that.

"Ready at last!" cried Kiku as the tailor bit off the
end of his thread. Rahul jumped to his feet. "Come on,
hurry up!" Kiku told him. She made her veil brush
over his face and teasingly trod on his foot. She burst
out laughing at her joke and could still be heard
laughing on the stairs.

Anjana went to her place at the bedroom window
to watch them leave. It·had rained during the day,
and now the evening was cool and moist. Crowds had
come out to enjoy a promenade by the sea, and with
the crowds came the beggars lucky enough to have
the sea-front for their beat : the man with the twisted
limbs who wound himself like a creeper round the
long pole he carried, the very respectable woman who
wore shoes and spoke English and hadn't eaten for
three days. Anjana saw a few crippled children
clinging to Rahul's car and tapping on the windows,
but Rahul swiftly drove off so that the children fell
back and hobbled as fast as they could to surround

some other car. The woman in the nursing-home opposite was at her post, her blank face gazing over the iron bars. She looked like a good housewife, enjoying a little respite from her duties after the day's chores. Probably she *had* been a good housewife — before she couldn't carry on any longer and her relatives had had to bring her here. Anjana understood how this could happen. She thought of poor Sultana — sitting at home in her horrible apartment, smoking and suffering, wearing youthful leopard pants — and asked herself, is it any wonder we go mad? She looked at the sky laid like a benediction over the housetops. The moon was up and there was one star. As usual, on seeing the sky, Anjana prayed : today not for Kiku and Rahul but for people who suffered — like herself, and Sultana, and Tara Bai. She prayed, her lips moving devoutly, her eyes upturned in humble supplication. But she didn't feel she was getting an answer.

She went to the telephone. Thakur Sahib answered himself and, at the sound of his voice, she was so overcome that she couldn't speak. "Hallo?" he said, twice, and "Hallo!" getting annoyed.

"Yes yes it's me," she said to him at last.

He grunted.

She shut her eyes, in bliss, in safety.

*   *   *

An Experience of India

Today Ramu left. He came to ask for money and I gave him as much as I could. He counted it and asked for more, but I didn't have it to give him. He said some insulting things, which I pretended not to hear. Really I couldn't blame him. I knew he was anxious and afraid, not having another job to go to. But I also couldn't help contrasting the way he spoke now with what he had been like in the past : so polite always, and eager to please, and always smiling, saying "Yes sir," "Yes madam please." He used to look very different too, very spruce in his white uniform and his white canvas shoes. When guests came, he put on a special white coat he had made us buy him. He was always happy when there were guests — serving, mixing drinks, emptying ashtrays — and I think he was disappointed that more didn't come. The Ford Foundation people next door had a round of buffet suppers and Sunday brunches, and perhaps Ramu suffered in status before their servants because we didn't have much of that. Actually, coming to think of it, perhaps he suffered in status anyhow because we weren't like the others. I mean, I wasn't. I didn't look like a proper memsahib or dress like one — I wore Indian clothes right from the start — or ever behave like one. I think perhaps Ramu didn't care for that. I think servants want their employers to be conventional and put up a good front so that other people's servants can respect them. Some of the nasty things Ramu told me this morning were about how everyone said I was just someone from a very low sweeper caste in my own country and how sorry they were for him that he had to serve such a person.

He also said it was no wonder Sahib had run away from me. Henry didn't actually run away, but it's true that things had changed between us. I suppose India made us see how fundamentally different we were from each other. Though when we first came, we both came we thought with the same ideas. We were both happy that Henry's paper had sent him out to India. We both thought it was a marvellous opportunity not only for him professionally but for both of us spiritually. Here was our escape from that Western materialism with which we were both so terribly fed up. But once he got here and the first enthusiasm had worn off, Henry seemed not to mind going back to just the sort of life we'd run away from. He even didn't seem to care about meeting Indians any more, though in the beginning he had made a great point of doing so; now it seemed to him all right to go only to parties given by other foreign correspondents and sit around there and eat and drink and talk just the way **they would** at home. After a while, I couldn't stand going with him any more, so we'd have a fight and then he'd go off by himself. That was a relief. I didn't want to be with any of those people and talk about inane things in their tastefully appointed airconditioned apartments.

I had come to India to *be* in India. I wanted to be changed. Henry didn't — he wanted a change, that's all, but not to be changed. After a while because of that he was a stranger to me and I felt I was alone, the way I'm really alone now. Henry had to travel a lot around the country to write his pieces, and in the beginning I used to go with him. But I didn't like the way he travelled, always by plane and staying in expensive hotels and drinking in the bar with the other correspondents. So I would leave him and go off by myself. I travelled the way everyone travels in India, just with a bundle and a roll of bedding which I could spread out anywhere and go to sleep. I went in third-class railway carriages and in those old lumbering buses that go from one small dusty town to another and are loaded with too many people inside and with too much scruffy baggage on top. At the end of my journeys, I emerged soaked in perspiration, soot, and dirt. I ate anything anywhere and always like everyone else with my fingers (I became good at that) — thick, half-raw chapattis from wayside stalls and little messes of lentils and vegetables served on a leaf, all the food the poor eat; sometimes if I didn't have anything, other people would share with me from out of their bundles. Henry, who had the usual phobia about bugs, said I would kill myself eating that way. But nothing ever happened. Once, in a desert fort in Rajasthan, I got very thirsty and asked the old caretaker to pull some water out of an ancient disused well for me. It was brown and sort of foul-smelling, and maybe there was a corpse in the well, who knows. But I was thirsty so I drank it, and still nothing happened.

People always speak to you in India, in buses and trains and on the streets, they want to know all about you and ask you a lot of personal questions. I didn't speak much Hindi, but somehow we always managed, and I didn't mind answering all those questions when I could. Women quite often used to touch me, run their hands over my skin just to feel what it was like I suppose, and they specially liked to touch my hair which is long and blonde. Sometimes I had several of them lifting up strands of it at the same time, one pulling this way and another that way and they would exchange excited comments and laugh and scream a lot; but in a nice way, so I couldn't help but laugh and scream with them. And people in India are so hospitable. They're always saying "Please come and stay in my house," perfect strangers that happen to be sitting near you on the train. Sometimes, if I didn't have any plans or if it sounded as if they might be living in an interesting place, I'd say "all right thanks," and I'd go along with them. I had some interesting adventures that way.

I might as well say straight off that many of these adventures were sexual. Indian men are very, very keen to sleep with foreign girls. Of course men in other countries are also keen to sleep with girls, but there's something specially frenzied about Indian men when they approach you. Frenzied and at the same time shy. You'd think that with all those ancient traditions they have — like the Kama Sutra, and the sculptures showing couples in every kind of position — you'd think that with all that behind them they'd be very highly skilled, but they're not. Just the opposite. Middle-aged men get as excited as a fifteen-year-old boy, and then of course they can't wait, they *jump* and before you know where you are, in a great rush, it's all over. And when it's over, it's over, there's nothing left. Then they're only concerned with getting away as soon as possible before anyone can find them out (they're always scared of being found out). There's no tenderness, no interest at all in the other person as a person; only the same kind of curiosity that there is on the buses and the same sort of questions are asked, like are you married, any children, why no children, do you like wearing our Indian dress . . . There's one question though that's not asked on the buses but that always inevitably comes up during sex, so that you learn to wait for it : always, at the moment of mounting excitement, they ask "How many men have you slept with?" and it's repeated over and over "How many? How many?" and then they shout "Aren't you ashamed?" and "Bitch!" — always that one word which seems to excite them more than any other, to call you that is the height of their love-making, it's the last frenzy, the final outrage : "Bitch!" Sometimes I couldn't stop myself but had to burst out laughing.

I didn't like sleeping with all these people, but I felt I had to. I felt I was doing good, though I don't know why, I couldn't explain it to myself. Only one of all those men ever spoke to me : I mean the way people having sex together are supposed to speak, coming near each other not only physically but also wanting to show each other what's deep inside them. He was a middle-aged man, a fellow-passenger on a bus, and we got talking at one of the stops the bus made at a way-side tea-stall. When he found I was on my way to X——— and didn't have anywhere to stay, he said, as so many have said before him, "Please come and stay in my house." And I said, as I had often said before, "All right." Only when we got there he didn't take me to his house but to a hotel. It was a very poky place in the bazaar and we had to grope our way up a steep smelly stone staircase and then there was a tiny room with just one string-cot and an earthenware water jug in it. He made a joke about there being only one bed. I was too tired to care much about anything. I only wanted to get it over with quickly and go to sleep. But afterwards I found it wasn't possible to go to sleep because there was a lot of noise coming up from the street where all the shops were still open though it was nearly midnight. People seemed to be having a good time and there was even a phonograph playing some cracked old love-song. My companion also couldn't get to sleep : he left the bed and sat down on the floor by the window and smoked one cigarette after the other. His face was lit up by the light coming in from the street outside and I saw he was looking sort of thoughtful and sad, sitting there smoking. He had rather a good face, strong bones but quite a feminine mouth and of course those feminine suffering eyes that most Indians have.

I went and sat next to him. The window was an arch reaching down to the floor so that I could see out into the bazaar. It was quite gay down there with all the lights; the phonograph was playing from the cold-drink shop and a lot of people were standing around there having highly-coloured pop-drinks out of bottles; next to it was a shop with pink and blue brassieres strung up on a pole. On top of the shops were wrought-iron balconies on which sat girls dressed up in tatty georgette and waving peacock fans to keep themselves cool. Sometimes men looked up to talk and laugh with them and they talked and laughed back. I realised we were in the brothel area; probably the hotel we were in was a brothel too.

I asked "Why did you bring me here?"

N

He answered "Why did you come?"

That was a good question. He was right. But I wasn't sorry I came. Why should I be? I said "It's all right. I like it."

He said "She likes it", and he laughed. A bit later he started talking : about how he had just been to visit his daughter who had been married a few months before. She wasn't happy in her in-laws' house, and when he said goodbye to her she clung to him and begged him to take her home. The more he reasoned with her, the more she cried, the more she clung to him. In the end he had had to use force to free himself from her so that he could get away and not miss his bus. He felt very sorry for her, but what else was there for him to do. If he took her away, her in-laws might refuse to have her back again and then her life would be ruined. And she would get used to it, they always did; for some it took longer and was harder, but they all got used to it in the end. His wife too had cried a lot during the first year of marriage.

I asked him whether he thought it was good to arrange marriages that way, and he looked at me and asked how else would you do it. I said something about love and it made him laugh and he said that was only for the films. I didn't want to defend my point of view; in fact, I felt rather childish and as if he knew a lot more about things than I did. He began to get amorous again, and this time it was much better because he wasn't so frenzied and I liked him better by now too. Afterwards he told me how when he was first married, he and his wife had shared a room with the whole family (parents and younger brothers and sisters), and whatever they wanted to do, they had to do very quickly and quietly for fear of anyone waking up. I had a strange sensation then, as if I wanted to strip off all my clothes and parade up and down the room naked. I thought of all the men's eyes that follow one in the street, and for the first time it struck me that the expression in them was like that in the eyes of prisoners looking through their bars at the world outside; and then I thought maybe I'm that world outside for them — the way I go here and there and talk and laugh with everyone and do what I like — maybe I'm the river and trees they can't have where they are. Oh, I felt so sorry, I wanted to do so much. And to make a start, I flung myself on my companion and kissed and hugged him hard, I lay on top of him, I smothered him, I spread my hair over his face because I wanted to make him forget everything that wasn't me — this room, his daughter, his wife, the women in georgette sitting on the balconies — I wanted everything to be new for him and as beautiful as I could make it. He liked it for a while but got tired quite quickly, probably because he wasn't all that young any more.

It was shortly after this encounter that I met Ahmed. He was eighteen years old and a musician. His family had been musicians as long as anyone could remember and the alley they lived in was full of other musicians, so that when you walked down it, it was like walking through a magic forest all lit up with music and sounds. Only there wasn't anything magic about the place itself which was very cramped and dirty; the houses were so old that, whenever there were heavy rains, one or two of them came tumbling down. I was never inside Ahmed's house or met his family — they'd have died of shock if they had got to know about me — but I knew they were very poor and scraped a living by playing at weddings and functions. Ahmed never had any money, just sometimes if he was lucky he had a few coins to buy his betel with. But he was cheerful and happy and enjoyed everything that came his way. He was married, but his wife was too young to stay with him and after the ceremony she had been sent back to live with her father who was a musician in another town.

When I first met Ahmed, I was staying in a hostel attached to a temple which was free of charge for pilgrims; but afterwards he and I wanted a place for us to go to, so I wired Henry to send me some more money. Henry sent me the money, together with a long complaining letter which I didn't read all the way through, and I took a room in a hotel. It was on the outskirts of town which was mostly waste land except for a few houses and some of these had never been finished. Our hotel wasn't finished either because the proprietor had run out of money, and now it probably never would be for the place had turned out to be a poor proposition, it was too far out of town and no one ever came to stay there. But it suited us fine. We had this one room, painted bright pink and quite bare except for two pieces of furniture — a bed and a dressing-table, both of them very shiny and new. Ahmed loved it, he had never stayed in such a grand room before; he bounced up and down on the bed which had a mattress and stood looking at himself from all sides in the mirror of the dressing-table.

I never in all my life was so gay with anyone the way I was with Ahmed. I'm not saying I never had a good time at home; I did. I had a lot of friends before I married Henry and we had parties and danced and drank and I enjoyed it. But it wasn't like with Ahmed because no one was ever as *carefree* as he was, as light and easy and just ready to play and live. At home we always had our problems, personal ones of course, but on top of those there were universal problems — social, and economic, and moral, we really cared about what was happening in the world around us and in our own minds, we felt a responsibility towards being here alive at this point in time and wanted to do our best. Ahmed had no thoughts like that at all; there wasn't a shadow on him. He had his personal problems from time to time, and when he had them, he was very downcast and sometimes he even cried. But they weren't anything really very serious — usually some family quarrel, or his father was angry with him — and they passed away, blew away like a breeze over a lake and left him sunny and sparkling again. He enjoyed everything so much : not only our room, and the bed and the dressing-table, and making love, but so many other things like drinking coca cola and spraying scent and combing my hair and my combing his; and he made up games for us to play like indoor cricket with a slipper for a bat and one of Henry's letters rolled up for a ball. He taught me how to crack his toes, which is such a great Indian delicacy, and yelled with pleasure when I got it right; but when he did it to me, I yelled with pain so he stopped at once and was terribly sorry. He was very considerate and tender. No one I've ever known was sensitive to my feelings as he was. It was like an instinct with him, as if he could feel right down into my heart and know what was going on there; and

without ever having to ask anything or my ever having
to explain anything, he could sense each change of
mood and adapt himself to it and feel with it. Henry
would always have to ask me "Now what's up? What's
the matter with you?" and when we were still all
right with each other, he would make a sincere effort
to understand. But Ahmed never had to make an
effort, and maybe if he'd had to he wouldn't have
succeeded because it wasn't ever with his mind that he
understood anything, it was always with his feelings.
Perhaps that was so because he was a musician and in
music everything is beyond words and explanations
anyway; and from what he told me about Indian music,
I could see it was very, very subtle, there are effects
that you can hardly perceive they're so subtle and
your sensibilities have to be kept tuned all the time to
the finest, finest point; and perhaps because of that
the whole of Ahmed was always at that point and he
could play me and listen to me as if I were his sarod.

After some time we ran out of money and Henry
wouldn't send any more, so we had to think what to
do. I certainly couldn't bear to part with Ahmed, and
in the end I suggested he'd better come back to Delhi
with me and we'd try and straighten things out with
Henry. Ahmed was terribly excited by the idea; he'd
never been to Delhi and was wild to go. Only it meant
he had to run away from home because his family
would never have allowed him to go, so one night he
stole out of the house with his sarod and his little
bundle of clothes and met me at the railway station.
We reached Delhi the next night, tired and dirty and
covered with soot the way you always get in trains
here. When we arrived home, Henry was giving a party;

not a big party, just a small informal group sitting around chatting. I'll never forget the expression on everyone's faces when Ahmed and I came staggering in with our bundles and bedding. My blouse had got torn in the train all the way down the side, and I didn't have a safety-pin so it kept flapping open and unfortunately I didn't have anything underneath. Henry's guests were all looking very nice, the men in smart bush-shirts and their wives in little silk cocktail dresses; and although after the first shock they all behaved very well and carried on as if nothing unusual had happened, still it was an awkward situation for everyone concerned.

Ahmed never really got over it. I can see now how awful it must have been for him, coming into that room full of strange white people and all of them turning round to stare at us. And the room itself must have been a shock to him, he can never have seen anything like it. Actually, it was quite a shock to me too. I'd forgotten that that was the way Henry and I lived. When we first came, we had gone to a lot of trouble doing up the apartment, buying furniture and pictures and stuff, and had succeeded in making it look just like the apartment we have at home except for some elegant Indian touches. To Ahmed it was all very strange. He stayed there with us for some time, and he couldn't get used to it. I think it bothered him to have so many *things* around, rugs and lamps and objets d'art; he couldn't see why they had to be there. Now that I had travelled and lived the way I had, I couldn't see why either; as a matter of fact I felt as if these things were a hindrance and cluttered up not only your room but your mind and your soul as well, hanging on them like weights.

We had some quite bad scenes in the apartment during those days. I told Henry that I was in love with Ahmed, and naturally that upset him, though what upset him most was the fact that he had to keep us both in the apartment. I also realised that this was an undesirable situation, but I couldn't see any way out of it because where else could Ahmed and I go? We didn't have any money, only Henry had, so we had to stay with him. He kept saying that he would turn both of us out into the streets but I knew he wouldn't. He wasn't the type to do a violent thing like that, and besides he himself was so frightened of the streets that he'd have died to think of anyone connected with him being out there. I wouldn't have minded all that much if he *had* turned us out : it was warm enough to sleep in the open and people always give you food if you don't have any. I would have preferred it really because it was so unpleasant with Henry; but I knew Ahmed would never have been able to stand it. He was quite a pampered boy, and though his family were poor, they looked after and protected each other very carefully; he never had to miss a meal or go dressed in anything but fine muslin clothes, nicely washed and starched by female relatives.

Ahmed bitterly repented having come. He was very miserable, feeling so uncomfortable in the apartment and with Henry making rows all the time. Ramu, the servant, didn't improve anything by the way he behaved, absolutely refusing to serve Ahmed and never losing an opportunity to make him feel inferior. Everything went out of Ahmed; he crumpled up as if he were a paper flower. He didn't want to play his sarod and he didn't want to make love to me, he just sat around with his head and his hands hanging down, and there were times when I saw tears rolling down his face and he didn't even bother to wipe them off. Although he was so unhappy in the apartment, he never left it and so he never saw any of the places he had been so eager to come to Delhi for, like the Juma Masjid and Nizamuddin's tomb. Most of the time he was thinking about his family. He wrote long letters to them in Urdu, which I posted, telling them where he was and imploring their pardon for running away; and long letters came back again and he read and read them, soaking them in tears and kisses. One night he got so bad he jumped out of bed and, rushing into Henry's bedroom, fell to his knees by the side of Henry's bed and begged to be sent back home again. And Henry, sitting up in bed in his pyjamas, said all right, in rather a lordly way I thought. So next day I took Ahmed to the station and put him on the train, and through the bars of the railway carriage he kissed my hands and looked into my eyes with all his old ardour and tenderness, so at the last moment I wanted to go with him but it was too late and the train pulled away out of the station and all that was left to me of Ahmed was a memory, very beautiful and delicate like a flavour or a perfume or one of those melodies he played on his sarod.

I became very depressed. I didn't feel like going travelling any more but stayed home with Henry and went with him to his diplomatic and other parties. He was quite glad to have me go with him again; he liked having someone in the car on the way home to talk to

about all the people who'd been at the party and
compare their chances of future success with his own.
I didn't mind going with him, there wasn't anything
else I wanted to do. I felt as if I'd failed at something.
It wasn't only Ahmed. I didn't really miss him all
that much and was glad to think of him back with his
family in that alley full of music where he was happy.
For myself I didn't know what to do next though I
felt that something still awaited me. Our apartment
led to an open terrace and I often went up there to
look at the view which was marvellous. The house we
lived in and all the ones around were white and pink
and very modern, with picture windows and little
lawns in front, but from up here you could look
beyond them to the city and the big mosque and the
fort. In between there were stretches of waste land,
empty and barren except for an occasional crumbly
old tomb growing there. What always impressed me
the most was the sky because it was so immensely big
and so unchanging in colour, and it made everything
underneath it — all the buildings, even the great fort,
the whole city, not to speak of all the people living
in it — seem terribly small and trivial and passing
somehow. But at the same time as it made me feel
small, it also made me feel immense and eternal. I
don't know, I can't explain, perhaps because it was
itself like that and this thought — that there *was*
something like that — made me feel that I had a part
in it, I too was part of being immense and eternal. It
was all very vague really and nothing I could ever speak
about to anyone; but because of it I thought well
maybe there is something more for me here after all.
That was a relief because it meant I wouldn't have to

go home and be the way I was before and nothing different or gained. For all the time, ever since I'd come and even before, I'd had this idea that there was something in India for me to *gain*, and even though for the time being I'd failed, I could try longer and at last perhaps I would succeed.

I'd met people on and off who had come here on a spiritual quest, but it wasn't the sort of thing I wanted for myself. I thought anything I wanted to find, I could find by myself travelling around the way I had done. But now that this had failed, I became interested in the other thing. I began to go to a few prayer-meetings and I liked the atmosphere very much. The meeting was usually conducted by a swami in a saffron robe who had renounced the world, and he gave an address about love and God and everyone sang hymns also about love and God. The people who came to these meetings were mostly middle-aged and quite poor. I had already met many like them on my travels, for they were the sort of people who sat waiting on station platforms and bus depots, absolutely patient and uncomplaining even when conductors and other officials pushed them around. They were gentle people and very clean though there was always some slight smell about them as of people who find it difficult to keep clean because they live in crowded and unsanitary places where there isn't much running water and the drainage system isn't good. I loved the expression that came into their faces when they sang hymns. I wanted to be like them, so I began to dress in plain white saris and I tied up my hair in a plain knot and the only ornament I wore was a string of beads not for decoration but to say the names of God on. I became a vegetarian and did my best to cast out all the undesirable human passions, such as anger and lust. When Henry was in an irritable or quarrelsome mood, I never answered him back but was very kind and patient with him. However, far from having a good effect, this seemed to make him worse. Altogether he didn't like the new personality I was trying to achieve but sneered a lot at the way I dressed and looked and the simple food I ate. Actually, I didn't enjoy this food very much and found it quite a trial eating nothing but boiled rice and lentils with him sitting opposite me having his cutlets and chops.

The peace and satisfaction that I saw on the faces of the other hymn-singers didn't come to me. As a matter of fact, I grew rather bored. There didn't seem much to be learned from singing hymns and eating vegetables. Fortunately just about this time someone took me to see a holy woman who lived on the roof of an old overcrowded house near the river. People treated her like a holy woman but she didn't set up to be one. She didn't set up to be anything really, but only stayed in her room on the roof and talked to people who came to see her. She liked telling stories and she could hold everyone spellbound listening to her, even though she was only telling the old mythological stories they had known all their lives long, about Krishna, and the Pandavas, and Rama and Sita. But she got terribly excited while she was telling them, as if it wasn't something that had happened millions of years ago but as if it was all real and going on exactly now. Once she was telling about Krishna's mother who made him open his mouth to see whether he had stolen and was eating up her butter. What did she seen then, inside his mouth?

"Worlds!" the holy woman cried. "Not just this world, not just one world with its mountains and rivers and seas, no, but world upon world, all spinning in one great eternal cycle in this child's mouth, moon upon moon, sun upon sun!"

She clapped her hands and laughed and laughed, and then she burst out singing in her thin old voice, some hymn all about how great God was and how lucky for her that she was his beloved. She was dancing with joy in front of all the people. And she was just a little shrivelled old woman, very ugly with her teeth gone and a growth on her chin : but the way she carried on it was as if she had all the looks and glamour anyone ever had in the world and was in love a million times over. I thought well whatever it was she had, obviously it was the one thing worth having and I had better try for it.

I went to stay with a guru in a holy city. He had a house on the river in which he lived with his disciples. They lived in a nice way : they meditated a lot and went out for boat rides on the river and in the evenings they all sat around in the guru's room and had a good time. There were quite a few foreigners among the disciples, and it was the guru's greatest wish to go abroad and spread his message there and bring back more disciples. When he heard that Henry was a journalist, he became specially interested in me. He talked to me about the importance of introducing the leaven of Indian spirituality into the lump of Western materialism. To achieve this end, his own presence in the West was urgently required, and to ensure the widest dissemination of his message he would also need the full support of the mass media. He said that since we live in the modern age, we must avail ourselves of all its resources. He was very keen for me to bring Henry into the ashram, and when I was vague in my answers — I certainly didn't want Henry here nor would he in the least want to come — he became very pressing and even quite annoyed and kept returning to the subject.

He didn't seem a very spiritual type of person to me. He was a hefty man with big shoulders and a big head. He wore his hair long but his jaw was clean-shaven and stuck out very large and prominent and gave him a powerful look like a bull. All he ever wore was a saffron robe and this left a good part of his body bare so that it could be seen at once how strong his legs and shoulders were. He had huge eyes which he used constantly and apparently to tremendous effect, fixing people with them and penetrating them with a steady beam. He used them on me when he wanted Henry to come, but they never did anything to me. But the other disciples were very strongly affected by them. There was one girl, Jean, who said they were like the sun, so strong that if she tried to look back at them something terrible would happen to her like being blinded or burned up completely.

Jean had made herself everything an Indian guru expects his disciples to be. She was absolutely humble and submissive. She touched the guru's feet when she came into or went out of his presence, she ran eagerly on any errand he sent her on. She said she gloried in being nothing in herself and living only by his will. And she looked like nothing too, sort of drained of everything she might once have been. At home her cheeks were probably pink but now she was quite white, waxen, and her hair too was completely faded and colourless. She always wore a plain white cotton sari and that made her look paler than ever, and thinner too, it seemed to bring out the fact that she had no hips and was utterly flat-chested. But she was happy — at least she said she was — she said she had never known such happiness and hadn't thought it was possible for human beings to feel like that. And when she said that, there was a sort of sparkle in her pale eyes, and at such moments I envied her because she seemed to have found what I was looking for. But at the same time I wondered whether she really had found what she thought she had, or whether it wasn't something else and she was cheating herself, and one day she'd wake up to that fact and then she'd feel terrible.

She was shocked by my attitude to the guru — not touching his feet or anything, and talking back to him as if he was just an ordinary person. Sometimes I thought perhaps there was something wrong with me because everyone else, all the other disciples and people from outside too who came to see him, they all treated him with this great reverence and their faces lit up in his presence as if there really was something special. Only I couldn't see it. But all the same I was quite happy there — not because of him, but because I liked the atmosphere of the place and the way they all lived. Everyone seemed very contented and as if they were living for something high and beautiful. I thought perhaps if I waited and was patient, I'd also come to be like that. I tried to meditate the way they all did, sitting crosslegged in one spot and concentrating on the holy word that had been given to me. I wasn't ever very successful and kept thinking of other things. But there were times when I went up to sit on the roof and looked out over the river, the way it stretched so calm and broad to the opposite bank and the boats going up and down it and the light changing and being reflected back on the water : and then, though I wasn't trying to meditate or come to any higher thoughts, I did feel very peaceful and was glad to be there.

The guru was patient with me for a long time, explaining about the importance of his mission and how Henry ought to come here and write about it for his paper. But as the days passed and Henry didn't show up, his attitude changed and he began to ask me questions. Why hadn't Henry come? Hadn't I written to him? Wasn't I going to write to him? Didn't I think what was being done in the ashram would interest him? Didn't I agree that it deserved to be brought to the notice of the world and that to this end no stone should be left unturned? While he said all this, he fixed me with his great eyes and I squirmed — not because of the way he was looking at me, but because I was embarrassed and didn't know what to answer. Then he became very gentle and said never mind, he didn't want to force me, that was not his way, he wanted people slowly to turn towards him of their own accord, to open up to him as a flower opens up and unfurls its petals and its leaves to the sun. But next day he would start again, asking the same questions, urging me, forcing me, and when this had gone on for some time and we weren't getting anywhere, he even got angry once or twice and shouted at me that I was obstinate and closed and had fenced in my heart with seven hoops of iron. When he shouted, everyone in the ashram trembled and afterwards they looked at me in a strange way. But an hour later the guru always had me called back to his room and then he was very gentle with me again and made me sit near him and insisted that it should be I who handed him his glass of milk in preference to one of the others, all of whom were a lot keener to be selected for this honour than I was.

Jean often came to talk to me. At night I spread my bedding in a tiny cubby-hole which was a disused store-room, and just as I was falling asleep, she would come in and lie down beside me and talk to me very softly and intimately. I didn't like it much, to have her so close to me and whispering in a voice that wasn't more than a breath and which I could feel, slightly warm, on my neck; sometimes she touched me, putting her hand on mine ever so gently so that she hardly was touching me but all the same I could feel that her hand was a bit moist and it gave me an unpleasant sensation down my spine. She spoke about the beauty of surrender, of not having a will and not having thoughts of your own. She said she too had been like me once, stubborn and ego-centred, but now she had learned the joy of yielding, and if she could only give me some inkling of the infinite bliss to be tasted in this process — here her breath would give out for a moment and she couldn't speak for ecstasy. I would take the opportunity to pretend to fall asleep, even snoring a bit to make it more convincing; after calling my name a few times in the hope of waking me up again, she crept away disappointed. But next night she'd be back again, and during the day too she would attach herself to me as much as possible and continue talking in the same way.

It got so that even when she wasn't there, I could

o

still hear her voice and feel her breath on my neck. I no longer enjoyed anything, not even going on the river or looking out over it from the top of the house. Although they hadn't bothered me before, I kept thinking of the funeral pyres burning on the bank, and it seemed to me that the smoke they gave out was spreading all over the sky and the river and covering them with a dirty yellowish haze. I realised that nothing good could come to me from this place now. But when I told the guru that I was leaving, he got into a great fury. His head and neck swelled out and his eyes became two coal-black demons rolling around in rage. In a voice like drums and cymbals, he *forbade* me to go. I didn't say anything but I made up my mind to leave next morning. I went to pack my things. The whole ashram was silent and stricken, no one dared speak. No one dared come near me either till late at night when Jean came as usual to lie next to me. She lay there completely still and crying to herself. I didn't know she was crying at first because she didn't make a sound but slowly her tears seeped into her side of the pillow and a sensation of dampness came creeping over to my side of it. I pretended not to notice anything.

Suddenly the guru stood in the doorway. The room faced an open courtyard and this was full of moonlight which illumined him and made him look enormous and eerie. Jean and I sat up. I felt scared, my heart beat fast. After looking at us in silence for a while, he ordered Jean to go away. She got up to do so at once. I said "No, stay," and clung to her hand but she disengaged herself from me and, touching the guru's feet in reverence, she went away. She seemed to dissolve in the moonlight outside, leaving no trace.

The guru sat beside me on my bedding spread on the floor. He said I was under a delusion, that I didn't really want to leave; my inmost nature was craving to stay by him — he knew, he could hear it calling out to him. But because I was afraid, I was attempting to smother this craving and to run away. "Look how you're trembling," he said. "See how afraid you are." It was true, I was trembling and cowering against the wall as far away from him as I could get. Only it was impossible to get very far because he was so huge and seemed to spread and fill the tiny closet. I could feel him close against me, and his pungent male smell, spiced with garlic, overpowered me.

"You're right to be afraid," he said : because it was his intention, he said, to batter and beat me, to smash my ego till it broke and flew apart into a million pieces and was scattered into the dust. Yes, it would be a painful process and I would often cry out and plead for mercy, but in the end — ah, with what joy I would step out of the prison of my own self, remade and reborn! I would fling myself to the ground and bathe his feet in tears of gratitude. Then I would be truly his. As he spoke, I became more and more afraid because I felt, so huge and close and strong he was, that perhaps he really had the power to do to me all that he said and that in the end he would make me like Jean.

I now lay completely flattened against the wall, and he had moved up and was squashing me against it. One great hand travelled up and down my stomach, but its activity seemed apart from the rest of him and from what he was saying. His voice became lower and lower, more and more intense. He said he would teach me to obey, to submit myself completely, that would be the first step and a very necessary one. For he knew what we were like, all of us who came from Western countries : we were self-willed, obstinate, *licentious.* On the last word his voice cracked with emotion, his hand went further and deeper. *Licentious*, he repeated, and then, rolling himself across the bed so that he now lay completely pressed against me, he asked "How many men have you slept with?" He took my hand and made me hold him : how huge and hot he was! He pushed hard against me. "How many? Answer me!" he commanded, urgent and dangerous. But I was no longer afraid : now he was not an unknown quantity nor was the situation any longer new or strange. "Answer me, answer me!" he cried, riding on top of me, and then he cried "Bitch!" and I laughed in relief.

I quite liked being back in Delhi with Henry. I had lots of baths in our marble bathroom, soaking in the tub for hours and making myself smell nice with bath-salts. I stopped wearing Indian clothes and took out all the dresses I'd brought with me. We entertained quite a bit, and Ramu scurried around in his white coat, emptying ashtrays. It wasn't a bad time. I stayed around all day in the apartment with the airconditioner on and the curtains drawn to keep out the glare. At night we drove over to other people's apartments for buffet suppers of boiled ham and potato salad; we sat around drinking in their living rooms, which were done up more or less like ours, and talked about things like the price of whisky, what was the best hill station to go to in the summer, and servants. This last subject often led to other related ones like how unreliable Indians were and how it was impossible ever to get anything done. Usually this subject was treated in a humorous way, with lots of funny anecdotes to illustrate, but occasionally someone got quite passionate; this happened usually if they were a bit drunk, and then they went off into a long thing about how dirty India was and backward, riddled with vile superstitions — evil, they said — corrupt — corrupting.

Henry never spoke like that — maybe because he never got drunk enough — but I know he didn't disagree with it. He disliked the place very much and was in fact thinking of asking for an assignment elsewhere. When I asked where, he said the cleanest place he could think of. He asked how would I like to go to Geneva. I knew I wouldn't like it one bit, but I said all right. I didn't really care where I was. I didn't care much about anything these days. The only positive feeling I had was for Henry. He was so sweet and good to me. I had a lot of bad dreams nowadays and was afraid of sleeping alone, so he let me come into his bed even though he dislikes having his sheets disarranged and I always kick and toss about a lot. I lay close beside him, clinging to him, and for the first time I was glad that he had never been all that keen on sex. On Sundays we stayed in bed all day reading the papers and Ramu brought us nice English meals on trays. Sometimes we put on a record and danced together in our pyjamas. I kissed Henry's cheeks which were always smooth — he didn't need to shave very often — and sometimes his lips which tasted of toothpaste.

Then I got jaundice. It's funny, all that time I spent

travelling about and eating anything anywhere, nothing happened to me, and now that I was living such a clean life with boiled food and boiled water, I got sick. Henry was horrified. He immediately segregated all his and my things, and anything that I touched had to be sterilised a hundred times over. He was for ever running into the kitchen to check up whether Ramu was doing this properly. He said jaundice was the most catching thing there was, and though he went in for a whole course of precautionary inoculations that had to be specially flown in from the States, he still remained in a very nervous state. He tried to be sympathetic to me, but couldn't help sounding reproachful most of the time. He had sealed himself off so carefully, and now I had let this in. I knew how he felt, but I was too ill and miserable to care. I don't remember ever feeling so *ill*. I didn't have any high temperature or anything, but all the time there was this terrible nausea. First my eyes went yellow, then the rest of me as if I'd been dyed in the colour of nausea, inside and out. The whole world went yellow and sick. I couldn't bear anything : any noise, any person near me, worst of all any smell. They couldn't cook in the kitchen any more because the smell of cooking made me scream. Henry had to live on boiled eggs and bread. I begged him not to let Ramu into my bedroom for, although Ramu always wore nicely laundered clothes, he gave out a smell of perspiration which was both sweetish and foul and filled me with disgust. I was convinced that under his clean shirt he wore a cotton vest, black with sweat and dirt, which he never took off but slept in at night in the one-room servant quarter where he lived crowded together with all his family in a dense smell of cheap food and bad drains and unclean bodies.

I knew these smells so well — I thought of them as the smells of India, and had never minded them; but now I couldn't get rid of them, they were like some evil flood soaking through the walls of my aircon- ditioned bedroom. And other things I hadn't minded, had hardly bothered to think about, now came back to me in a terrible way so that waking and sleeping I saw them. What I remembered most often was the disused well in the Rajasthan fort out of which I had drunk water. I was sure now that there had been a corpse at the bottom of it, and I saw this corpse with the flesh swollen and blown but the eyes intact : they were huge like the guru's eyes and they stared, glazed and jellied, into the darkness of the well. And worse than seeing this corpse, I could taste it in the water that I had drunk — that I was still drinking — yes, it was now, at this very moment, that I was raising my cupped hands to my mouth and feeling the dank water lap around my tongue. I screamed out loud at the taste of the dead man and I called to Henry and clutched his hand and begged him to get us sent to Geneva quickly, quickly. He disengaged his hand — he didn't like me to touch him at this time — but he promised. Then I grew calmer, I shut my eyes and tried to think of Geneva and of washing out my mouth with Swiss milk.

I got better, but I was very weak. When I looked at myself in the mirror, I started to cry. My face had a yellow tint, my hair was limp and faded; I didn't look old but I didn't look young any more either. There was no flesh left, and no colour. I was drained, hollowed out. I was wearing a white night-dress and that

increased the impression. Actually, I reminded myself
of Jean. I thought so this is what it does to you (I
didn't quite know at that time what I meant by it —
jaundice in my case, a guru in hers; but it seemed to
come to the same). When Henry told me that his new
assignment had come through, I burst into tears again;
only now it was with relief. I said let's go now, let's go
quickly. I became quite hysterical so Henry said all
right; he too was impatient to get away before any
more of those bugs he dreaded so much caught up
with us. The only thing that bothered him was that
the rent had been paid for three months and the landlord refused to refund. Henry had a fight with him
about it but the landlord won. Henry was furious but
I said never mind, let's just get away and forget all
about all of them. We packed up some of our belong-
ings and sold the rest; the last few days we lived in an
empty apartment with only a couple of kitchen chairs
and a bed. Ramu was very worried about finding a
new job.

   Just before we were to leave for the airport and
were waiting for the car to pick us up, I went on the
terrace. I don't know why I did that, there was no
reason. There was nothing I wanted to say goodbye
to, and no last glimpses I wanted to catch. My thoughts
were all concentrated on the coming journey and
whether to take air-sickness pills or not. The sky from
up on the terrace looked as immense as ever, the city
as small. It was evening and the light was just fading
and the sky wasn't any definite colour now : it was
sort of translucent like a pearl but not an earthly
pearl. I thought of the story the little saintly old
woman had told about Krishna's mother and how

she saw the sun and the moon and world upon world in his mouth. I liked that phrase so much — world upon world — I imagined them spinning around each other like glass balls in eternity and everything as shining and translucent as the sky I saw above me. I went down and told Henry I wasn't going with him. When he realised — and this took some time — that I was serious, he knew I was mad. At first he was very patient and gentle with me, then he got in a frenzy. The car had already arrived to take us. Henry yelled at me, he grabbed my arm and began to pull me to the door. I resisted with all my strength and sat down on one of the kitchen chairs. Henry continued to pull and now he was pulling me along with the chair as if on a sleigh. I clung to it as hard as I could but I felt terribly weak and was afraid I would let myself be pulled away. I begged him to leave me. I cried and wept with fear — fear that he would take me, fear that he would leave me.

Ramu came to my aid. He said it's all right Sahib, I'll look after her. He told Henry that I was too weak to travel after my illness but later, when I was better, he would take me to the airport and put me on a plane. Henry hesitated. It was getting very late, and if he didn't go, he too would miss the plane. Ramu assured him that all would be well and Henry need not worry at all. At last Henry took my papers and ticket out of his inner pocket. He gave me instructions how I was to go to the air company and make a new booking. He hesitated a moment longer — how sweet he looked all dressed up in a suit and tie ready for travelling, just like the day we got married — but the car was hooting furiously downstairs and he had to go.

I held on hard to the chair. I was afraid if I didn't I might get up and run after him. So I clung to the chair, trembling and crying. Ramu was quite happily dusting the remaining chair. He said we would have to get some more furniture. I think he was glad that I had stayed and he still had somewhere to work and live and didn't have to go tramping around looking for another place. He had quite a big family to support.

I sold the ticket Henry left with me but I didn't buy any new furniture with it. I stayed in the empty rooms by myself and very rarely went out. When Ramu cooked anything for me, I ate it, but sometimes he forgot or didn't have time because he was busy looking for another job. I didn't like living like that but I didn't know what else to do. I was afraid to go out : everything I had once liked so much — people, places, crowds, smells — I now feared and hated. I would go running back to be by myself in the empty apartment. I felt people looked at me in a strange way in the streets; and perhaps I was strange now from the way I was living and not caring about what I looked like any more; I think I talked aloud to myself sometimes — once or twice I heard myself doing it. I spent a lot of the money I got from the air ticket on books. I went to the bookshops and came hurrying back carrying armfuls of them. Many of them I never read, and even those I did read, I didn't understand very much. I hadn't had much experience in reading these sort of books — like the Upanishads and the Vedanta Sutras — but I liked the sound of the words and I liked the feeling they gave out. It was as if I were all by myself on an immensely high plateau breathing in great lungfuls of very sharp, pure air. Sometimes the landlord came to see what I was doing. He went round all the rooms, peering suspiciously into corners, testing the fittings. He kept asking how much longer I was going to stay; I said till the three months rent was up. He brought prospective tenants to see the apartment, but when they saw me squatting on the floor in the empty rooms, sometimes with a bowl of half-eaten food which Ramu had neglected to clear away, they got nervous and went away again rather quickly. After a time the electricity got cut off because I hadn't paid the bill. It was very hot without the fan and I filled the tub with cold water and sat in it all day. But then the water got cut off too. The landlord came up twice, three times a day now. He said if I didn't clear out the day the rent was finished he would call the police to evict me. I said it's all right, don't worry, I shall go. Like the landlord, I too was counting the days still left to me. I was afraid what would happen to me.

Today the landlord evicted Ramu out of the servant quarter. That was when Ramu came up to ask for money and said all those things. Afterwards I went up on the terrace to watch him leave. It was such a sad procession. Each member of the family carried some part of their wretched household stock, none of which looked worth taking. Ramu had a bed with tattered strings balanced on his head. In two days time I too will have to go with my bundle and my bedding. I've done this so often before — travelled here and there without any real destination — and been so happy doing it; but now it's different. That time I had a great sense of freedom and adventure. Now I feel compelled, that I *have* to do this whether I want to or not. And partly I don't want to, I feel afraid. Yet it's still like an adventure, and that's why besides being afraid I'm also excited, and most of the time I don't know why my heart is beating fast, is it in fear or in excitement, wondering what will happen to me now that I'm going travelling again.

*   *   *